High Tide

By

Denise Irwin

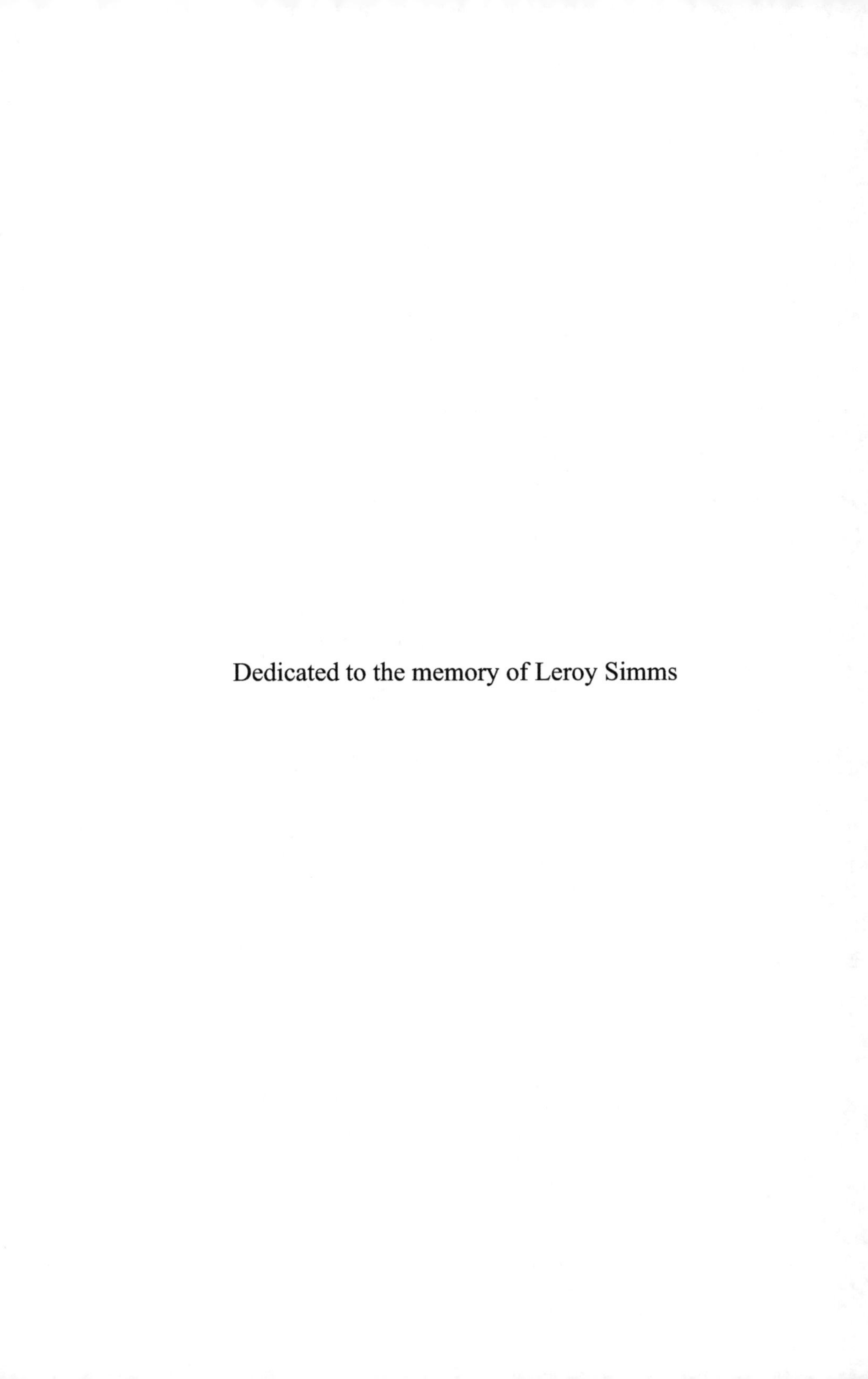

Dedicated to the memory of Leroy Simms

Chapter One

Skye and Malcom Stanford had been working on plans for over a year to sail to St. Thomas and live on the boat. That day was fast approach, so they hustled to get everything together to leave in mid-March on their 40' center cockpit Endeavor named The Jolly Roger to avoid the hurricane weather that starts in June.

Malcom is a medium height man, who stands at 5'11" tall with brown hair that is just starting to recede on his forehead giving anyone the opportunity to see his twinkling brown eyes better. He had sailed all his life from the time he was just a small boy and had sailed to the Islands many times with his parents. His wife Skye had never sailed until she met Malcom.

Sky is a short woman wiry woman standing 5'2" tall and at 40 years old wore her brown hair cropped to match her brown sparkling eyes. She'd never sailed before she met Malcom. Their first date was an evening sail on Middle River with a J-24 that he raced. She fell in love with both Malcom and sailing that night.

A week before they were scheduled to leave, Skye' parents threw a bon voyage party for them. The partiers filled the house and spread out onto the lawn. The music was playing so everyone danced after a plate of food along with a healthy amount of libation. Several folks asked if they flew over, could they stay on the boat. Malcom and Skye told them that they would be welcome. Malcom was secretly hoping that they didn't come at the same time.

He then heard Skye say, "The more the merrier and if we end up with too many merry makers there are hotels near the dock."

The farewell party lasted until dawn. Many stayed to help clean up and spend a few last minutes together to give out hugs and kisses before leaving.

The sun was on the horizon as they drove home. Skye asked, "Did someone sell tickets to our bon voyage party, because I saw folks that I've never met before."

"I saw them as well, and figured they were friends of friends or were just wandering around and heard the racket from the music and came in to see what was going on."

They were set to leave but figured it wouldn't hurt to check to make sure. Skye's parents were going to take care of the house and pay the bills from her primary checking and they would live off Malcolm's account and the money they had tucked away. Malcom had worked as an investment counselor and Skye as an attorney, so living frugally had given them the chance to retire early and live on the boat. They had considered selling the house and stash the cash but decided not to do that just yet. Skye's mother had a power of attorney if they changed their minds.

They decided to sleep on the boat the night before their departure on the 11th and leave after breakfast. They were eating breakfast in the cockpit when a contingent walked down the pier on the pretense of casting off the lines for them. Everyone was invited onboard for cup of coffee. Skye's parent brought bottle of champagne to bring in the New Year. Their well-wishers stepped on the dock to take up their post to cast the lines off.

Malcom sounded the horn, and everyone waved goodbye as they slid out of the slip at Markley's Marina. The wind was out of the west, so Malcolm motored out of Middle River while Sky did the KP for the breakfast dishes as well as the coffee cups their well-wishers had used.

Once they cleared the dyke, the sails were set they had a comfortable sail down the Bay, enjoying the warm sunshine and the brisk air that kept the sails full. Skye put lunch together and brought it out to the cockpit. While Malcom did the KP, Skye took the helm and let out a gut yell, "Wahoo."

Malcom brought a book out to read in the cockpit and was rocked to sleep with the boat's movement in the small waves slapping against the haul.

The air died at dusk which wasn't unusual for the Bay, so they drifted along and had dinner in the cockpit. Skye did the KP and then joined her husband in the cockpit as they enjoyed the stars overhead lighting the water up.

The Jolly Roger had drifted south on the outgoing tide to the Smith Island where a runabout motored close to them. There were two young men onboard and one asked if they needed help.

Malcom said, "Thank you, but we're doing fine, just enjoying the cool evening."

One of the guys from the runabout climbed up onto the Jolly Rogers deck and told Malcom and Skye to go below in the cabin and stabbed both of them there. He pushed their dead bloody bodies to the cabin sole and set about moving blocks of cocaine from the runabout to the Jolly Roger. They cut open one of the blocks to test the quality and once they were satisfied with the quality, shot holes in the bottom of the runabout to sink it.

One of the drug dealers asked, "Are we gonna throw the bodies overboard?"

The other one said, "No, because we don't want anyone to find them. After we offload the drugs to the cruiser, we'll open the scuppers in the cabin and let it sink. We'll be long gone if anyone finds the sunken sailboat.

One of the drug runners appointed himself as the leader, so he took the wheel to motor the Jolly Roger to Smith Island where they offloaded the cocaine to a 40' cabin cruiser. After which they went below and opened all the scuppers so she would sink.

The Jolly Roger was more resilient than they knew because while taking water through the open scuppers filling the cabin with bay water, she managed to drift south on the outgoing tide and ground herself on the Tangier Island beach

A fisherman on his way for the day saw the grounded sailboat and radioed the Coast Guard to alert them about it.

Someone from the James Park Marina towed the Jolly Roger to the marina and secured her in a slip.

Milton Park, who had inherited the marina from his father was a tall man, standing 6'2" with a solid frame from working in the yard all his life, had a casual attitude until he found the two dead bodies in the cabin floor where the blood mixed with incoming water giving it a pinkish hue. He went below and carefully worked around the bodies to close the scuppers. He then placed a call to the FBI's Marine Forensic Specialist. He had worked with her before and knew she was one fine looking woman standing at 5'7" tall with shorter blonde hair and he had to keep his yard workers away from her, because she was built like a brick shithouse.

It was a long trip to reach the James Park Marine on the Tangier Island. She left home to drive to Crisfield, Maryland on the Eastern Shore. She left her car in Crisfield and took a ferry to the Tangier Island.

Milton greeted her as soon as she stepped off the Ferry, "Ms. Brock, it is so good to see you and I'm sure you can help us with what now is a mystery."

"Milton, please call me Sophie. Has anything been moved on the boat?"

"I closed the scuppers, so the water stopped coming in and the fisherman who found them transported the bodies to Crisfield. One of the three Medical Examiners will give us a report."

She and the owner went below and walked in what was left of the water. Sophie hoped to find something that would give her a reason why the owners were found dead in the boat. The remaining water was pink, an indication for her that they had bled out a lot of blood. She moved to the NAV station to find information on the victims. She found the Coast Guard certificate indicating that the boat was owned by Skye and Malcom Stanford. The address was 2907 Manns Avenue, Parkville. Maryland 21234. Paid invoices for Markley's Marina were found in the paperwork.

In her search, she found was appeared to be traces where boxes were set on the boat's galley counter while it was transported to somewhere else. She found a trace of cocaine, probably used by the folks who killed the owners she dusted for fingerprints and would have them sent to her office in DC for analysis.

"Milton, is there a drug problem here on the Island?"

He told her, "I've heard nothing about drugs here on our small island, but I have heard that Smith Island has a problem. It could be just a rumor, but it might be worth checking out."

"Milton thanks you for all your help today. I'm gonna head out now and will let you know what I learn."

"Sophie, what should I do with the boat?"

"If you can haul her here in your yard, I'll be back to tell you what we can do. Here, this is my card it has my cell number on it."

She caught the last Ferry to Crisfield and was delighted that the Medical Examiner's Office was still open. Stephen Mears was the only one left in the building.

Sophie introduced herself, "Good evening, my name is Sophie Brock and I work for the FBI in the Marine Forensic Crime."

"Ms. Brock, how may I help you?"

"Skye and Malcom Stanford were murder victims on their boat. I was told they were brought here for an autopsy and hoped you could share with me what you learned."

"Of course, I can. Both were stabbed but that didn't kill them; they bled to death."

Sophie was horrified by what Mears just told her but before she could leave, she asked, "Did you find any evidence of drugs in their systems?"

"No. Were you looking for something specific?"

"I found traces of cocaine in the boat."

"That may have been from the murderers. Off the record, my opinion is that these guys were either new at this or too stupid to know what to do. It's been my experience that a good drug trafficker throws the body overboard and let the fish eat them to take away the existence that there were folks murdered."

"Dr. Mears, it's been a long day so I'm going to give you my card. Call me if you learn something new or need to ask me a question."

"Ms. Brock, before you go, if you managed to get some fingerprints from the boat, the Crisfield Forensic Lab can run them for you."

"I'll do that in the morning. Thank you because that saves me a great deal of time."

She left and drove to the Tawesmore Inn hoping it had a room available. They did, so she took her belongings to her room and found it to be more than she expected. The rooms were beautiful, and the large front porch held rocking chairs and the grounds were well tended to. Her next task was to find a place for dinner. The hotel receptionist suggested the Waterman's Inn.

Knowing that she was in crab country, she ordered the handmade crab cake with a side salad along with a glass of wine.

She made her way back to the Tawesmore Inn and slept until morning

<>

Sophie woke feeling refreshed after a good night of sleep. She showered and dressed and then made her way to the Inn's dining room for breakfast. She wasn't surprised that breakfast was great, because everything she'd eaten in Crisfield was worth coming back to eat again.

She drove to the Crisfield Police Department where she met with Chief Tim Willoughby, who stood 6' tall with short cropped blonde hair. Rather than wearing a uniform, he wore a genuinely nice suit that fit him as though it was made on him.

She explained the situation to him, "My name is Sophie Brock and I work for the FBI in the Marine Crime Forensic lab."

I'm currently in pursuit of a person or persons who murdered the owners on their boat. I have fingerprints from the countertop along with a substance I believe might a trace of cocaine. Is there any way that you might be able to help me?"

"We have a forensic lab here in the building, so let's take everything to them and grab a cup of coffee while waiting for the results."

He drove them to a coffee shop named The Gathering Place and as soon as she walked through the door, it as though you were walking into someone's home, where they had great coffee.

Tim asked her, "How did you end up in your job?"

"I studied marine biology in college hoping to make a difference in the waters' eco system. I found what I considered to be criminal acts like folks throwing trash and human waste overboard to end up killing the marine life. I found hashish oil floating on the water and asked if I could include drug trafficking to my list. It was approved, so here I am still trying to make a difference. It's your turn, how did you become the Police Chief in Crisfield?"

"I grew up in Crisfield the marine life poaching always bothered me; fisherman would fish for out of season fish and crabs and take them to the western shore where no one cared whether they were caught in season or out of season."

Sophie said, "That's amazing. We live miles away from one another and learn that our goals and aspirations aren't vastly different."

"I can't disagree with that." He blushed before he said, "I think it's time to check on what the lab has."

He drove them back to the station where her prints and photos were ready.

The first set was for George Patrick, who had a baby face with cropped blonde hair and looked as though he hasn't graduated from high school yet.

The second set was for Harold Simms, who looked as though he also hadn't graduated from high school yet.

"Tim, I'm dismayed by their age."

"I can't disagree with that. Are you still planning to take the ferry to Smith Island?"

"Now, more than ever, I need to go and find out who is using children to traffic drugs."

"Sophie, just remember that I'm the Police Chief for Smith Island and that means call me if you need me."

"I will. How late will you be here?"

"I'll stay in the office until you return, and we can talk about your day over dinner."

She took the ferry to Smith Island with her prints and photos in her case. She walked to the Smith Island Marina to speak with the Manager, Jason York, who turned out to be a tall thin young man with long tangled blonde hair and smelled as though he hadn't bathed in days, or maybe weeks.

"My name is Sophie Brock and I work with the FBI's Marine Criminal Forensic Lab."

After she introduced herself, she cringed when he wanted to shake her hand. While she knew that she had to do this her stomach rolled over pushing bile into her throat. She gave him a quick shake and pulled the paperwork from her hoping that there was a wash basin close to wash her hands. She could be wrong, but this guy looked as though he wasn't the brightest bulb in the pack, so she started with the photos first figuring pictures might work better than words. She showed him the photos first and asked, "Do you know the names of the folks in these photos?"

Without hesitation, he told her, "Nope."

Sophie worded her question a bit differently, "Have you ever worked with or seen the folks hanging around in the photos?"

"I told you 'no' before and I guess that I have to repeat myself, 'No – NO', I have no idea who those photos are of."

"Mr. York, please take a look at these two RAP sheets, do you now have any idea who they are? They both have a history of dealing drugs."

"Lady, I told you before that I didn't know them and I ain't gonna repeat myself again."

"In that case, would you mind, if I took a quick look around?"

"Not without a without a warrant, so you can just get yourself out of here."

She knew if she went back to Crisfield to get a warrant, this place would be clean and ready for inspection, so she decided to change her course of action. These two young men are wanted for both drug trafficking and two counts of murder. I can add you to the charges."

"Lady, I already told you that I don't know those two guys, so go and get your warrant."

Against her better judgment, she said, "Thank you for your help. I'm going to catch the last ferry to Crisfield. Call me if you remember something about the two guys in the photos." She handed him her card and left to catch the last ferry of the day to Crisfield.

When she exited the ferry; Sophie updated Tim on her day and then said that she had to drive to Maryland in the morning to let Skye's parents know that Skye and Malcom were murdered in the boat and bring them to Crisfield to identify the bodies.

Tim said, "Sophie, you're tired and need a good meal followed by a night of restful sleep before you drive to Maryland, so why don't we have dinner at the Waterman' Inn and then I can drive you back to the Inn to sleep. During dinner Tim said that he would take the ferry to Smith Island to keep an eye on York while she drove to Maryland"

<>

Sophie was up early, had breakfast in the Inn; however, before leaving for Maryland, she decided to call Skye's parents, Helen, and Fred. Knowing that calling them would destroy them she made the call.

Her father answered the call and asked, "May I help you?"

"My name is Sophie Broke and I work for the FBI in the Marine Forensic Crime lab. Your daughter and her husband were murdered on their boat."

"Can you please hold for a moment?"

"Of course, I can."

She could hear Mr. Barton explain to his wife the nature of the call and when he returned to the call with Sophie, he asked, "Where are our daughter and son-in-law?"

"They are currently in the Crisfield Mortuary. I would like to offer you that I'll come and pick the two of you up and bring you to Crisfield."

"Ms. Brock, thank you for the offer, but we know the way. Since it's a long drive, we'll see you tomorrow if it's okay with you."

"It is absolutely okay with me. Would you like for me to make hotel reservations for you? I'm staying at the Tawesmore Inn, which is quite nice, and I can make reservations for you."

"Again, Ms. Brock, thank you for the offer. My wife is on the phone as we speak, making reservations at the Inn."

"If I can be of any help, please call me at 800-555-5555. I'll meet you in the lobby of the Police Station tomorrow."

Her next call was to Tim, "I called Skye's parents and they'll be here sometime tomorrow and already made reservations for the Tawesmore Inn."

"That sounds good, have you eaten yet?"

"I had breakfast at the Inn and then made the call to Barton's."

"Are you up for something other than the Waterman Inn?"

"What do you have in mind?"

"We have a place here in Crisfield called Bubbas Wing Shack. Wings are served in a variety of sauce choices."

"Well, that sounds like an interesting place to go, so lead on."

He parked this car on the lot, and they entered through the front door. The hostess told them, "It's a two-hour wait for a table, but there are a few open spots at the bar."

Tim looked to Sophie to make the decision. She said, "We're here, so the bar is fine as long as they don't serve us snack food."

The hostess assured her that the menu for the tables is available at the bar.

Tim ordered their beverages and when they came, he asked, "Would you mind if I ordered the food?"

"Not at all, so order away."

Tim ordered a variety of the flavored wings.

Sophie really liked that she could eat the wings with her fingers and listened to how his day went on Smith Island.

"The owner, Toby Wilhelm, told me that he fired York this morning because he had his hand in the candy jar taking his portion of the drug deal in cocaine."

"Tim. Does that mean we've lost everything we put together for an arrest?"

"No. because Toby's gonna get involved and see who's looking for York to make another drug deal."

"That sure helps us if the owner is gonna help."

"I'm glad to hear that we're on the same page. I need to get you to your hotel to get some sleep before the Barton's arrive tomorrow.

<>

After a night of restful sleep, Sophie was up early ready to face the day. She showered and dressed and then went down for breakfast and then wasn't sure wasn't sure what she would do next. She was on hold until the Barton's arrive. She put her cell phone into her coat pocket and when out for a walk on a sunny but windy morning.

The walk cleared her mind, so she could think. She now knew what she would say to the Barton's when they arrived at some time today. The sun ducked behind some low dark clouds and that encourage her to get back to the Inn before she was rained on.

She entered through the front door and found Tim in the lobby drinking a cup of coffee.

He looked up and saw her, "Good morning Sophie, I figured you were antsy about the Barton's arrive and could use some company."

"I went out for a walk and that didn't help, so I'm happy to see you here. There are so many questions running through my head that I'm getting confused."

"Well, let's see if we can work on that by putting some framework together. What's the most important item to you?"

"Find our suspects before they arrive."

"Since it's likely that won't happen, what's next?"

"Show them the photos with their names on it and last is the boat."

"Sophie, it's likely they will need to decide about the boat."

Her cell phone rang; the call was from Fred Barton, who told her, "We're about an hour out. The traffic has made it slow going."

"Don't worry about that, Tim and I will meet you in the station."

She updated Tim about the call from Fred Barton and he suggested, "In that case let's head to the station so we're there before them."

Sophie followed Tim to the station to find that Helen and Fred were there and after the round of introductions, they asked if they could see and identify Skye and Malcom.

The four of them made their way down to the morgue where the Barton's confirmed that it was their daughter and her husband.

Mr. Barton asked, "Is there was a quiet place in the station where we can make arrangements to bring them home."

Tim showed them to his office. He and Sophie waited quietly outside in the squad room.

When Helen and Fred Barton came out of his office, Fred said, "That's done, and the boat can wait until tomorrow."

Tim asked, "Do you have reservations for dinner?"

"We reserved a table for four at the Waterman Inn hoping that you and Ms. Brock can join us."

Tim nodded to Sophie, who nodded back. Tim said, "We'll meet you there."

They arrived at the same time and parked side by side by side. Fred had reserved a table for four and as they sat a waitress appeared to give them menus and take drink orders. She returned to deliver their beverages and took their dinner orders.

Fred asked, "Has there been any headway on who murdered Skye and Malcom?"

Sophie pulled the paperwork out of her bag. "There were fingerprints in the cabin and the Crisfield Forensic Lab was able to not only find a match, they also had photos of them. She handed them the paperwork as she said, "I made a copy for you to keep. Someone may have tipped them off and in my opinion and this is just my opinion; it was the Marina Manager on Smith Island, because they are both missing. I put out an APB on both."

Helen said, "They look so young to be guilty of murder."

"Helen, I agree with you that they look young; however, that doesn't make them any less criminal in their behavior. I found traces of cocaine on the galley counter which means they tapped into one of packs intended for sale."

"That's just awful. I don't understand how boys so young could do such a thing."

Fred said, "Things have changed since we raised Skye."

There were tears in her eyes when she responded, "They sure have."

Fred asked, "Sophie have you been back to the boat yet?"

"No, but I can call the marina owner and learn what shape She's in."

Fred asked, "Can the two of you join Helen and me to go to the marina tomorrow?"

Sophie and Tim both said that they could. Everyone agreed to meet for breakfast in the Tawesmore Inn and then take the ferry to Tangiers Island.

<>

After a hearty breakfast in the Inn, everyone drove to the ferry landing, parked their cars, and took the ferry to Tangiers Island.

The foursome walked to the James Park Marina where Milton Park gave them a warm greeting and then said, "The boat was hauled, and my cleaning crew cleaned it so that it could get put back in the water."

Fred asked, "Mr. Park, can I go up the ladder and get a look at the interior?"

"Of course, you can."

The interior was spic and span clean. Everything shined to look brand new.

He told Milton, "I'll give you a call after I put a crew together to bring the Jolly Roger home to the Middle River. What's the current storage fee that I owe you?"

"Fred, you don't have a storage fee in my marina, but I'd like to make you an offer. I can sell the boat as a charter boat and you don't have to find a crew to sail it to Middle River, unless of course there's someone who wants the boat."

"Milton, please excuse Helen and I for a moment to talk over your offer."

They stepped to the side to discuss the offer. Helen said, "Fred, we can walk away from the insurance, maintenance and slip fees today. There's no one in Maryland who's gonna want the boat."

Fred said, "Milton, we're happy to accept your offer."

"Fred, I'll call you when she's sold and mail you half of the proceeds. The other half I'll keep, to pay the cleaning crew."

Fred handed him his card and shook his hand before he said, "Milton, thank you, that's a huge monkey off our backs."

<>

They made their way back to Crisfield on the ferry.

Tim asked, "Do you have time for lunch before you go?

"Helen said, "That would be great."

Fred asked, "Where are we going?"

Tim said, "Bubbas Wing Shack."

Helen said, "Oh my word, is that place still open; we used to eat there every time we came to Crisfield."

The conversation was casual during lunch.

Fred gave Sophie his card and asked, "Sophie, can you keep us up to date on the suspects?"

"Of course, I will."

Fred paid the bill and after a round of thank you, the Barton's were on their way home.

Tim drove Sophie to the hotel and said, "I guess you'll be heading home tomorrow."

"Not with an unsolved murder."

Chapter Two

Sophie came down for breakfast and found Tim sipping on a cup of coffee.

She said, "Good Morning Tim, let me grab a cup of coffee join you."

When she returned with her cup of coffee, he asked, "Do you have an idea about how you're going to use to find your suspects?"

"I thought of nothing else all night. My plan is to get a room in the Bayside Inn and Restaurant and sit at the bar to hear and see what I can hoping that I might get a lead Of course I'll also keep in touch with Toby Wilhelm and work with him to find my bandits."

Tim asked, "Sophie, can I make a suggestion that we have dinner together either on Smith Island or in Crisfield so that we can keep one another updated?"

"Tim, I would really like that, because it's a great idea."

"I hoped you would." Tim then picked up her bag and walked with her to the ferry landing. He gave her bag back to her as he said, "Sophie, call me if you need me or run into problems."

As she stepped onto the ferry, Sophie said, "I will."

She waved goodbye as the ferry pulled away from the dock. Tim waved goodbye and stood to watch the ferry until it was out of sight. He shook his head hoping the best for her and then walked back to the station.

It was a windy day, so the ferry did a little rock and rolling in the building waves. She saw that a few of its travelers looked a little green around the gills.

<>

When the ferry docked, Sophie walked to the Bayside Inn to check in and once that was done, she walked to the Smith Island Marina to meet Toby Wilhelm, the owner. His office sat just off the parking lot before the piers giving him a birds-eye view of the parking lot and the piers. The door was open, so she tapped on it before going in.

He looked up from his desk and asked, "How can I help you Miss?"

"My name is Sophie Brock and I work for the FBI's Marine Crime Lab. I'm investigating the murder of Skye and Malcom Stanford aboard their Endeavor. I was able to get two things off the boat, the first was fingerprints and the second was a trace of cocaine left on the boat's galley countertop."

Sophie pulled the photos from her bag and handed them to Wilhelm, as she said, "These are the two that I'm looking have you seen either one?"

"No, I haven't Agent Brock, but if I do, I'll call."

She handed him her card as she said, "I'm staying at the Bayside Inn."

"I'll keep my eyes and ears open because I just fired my manager who didn't do just that."

She called Tim to let him know her day went, but before she could say anything he said, "I'm on my way to have dinner with you."

"Tim you know better than me that the ferry has stopped running for the day."

"Sophie, you are right because the ferry has stopped running for the day, but I'll let you in on a little secret. I have a boat, which means that I'm not dependent on the ferry schedule."

She said, "Wow, I didn't know that you have a boat. I'm staying at the Bayside Inn, so I'll meet you at the bar in the restaurant."

"Don't get all slopped up before I get there."

"Then don't waste time getting here."

◇

Sophie was sitting at the bar when Tim arrived; he sat beside her and ordered a drink. When he had his Heineken draft sitting in front of him, he asked, "Did you learn anything new and useful today?"

She shook her head as she said, "No, not a damn thing, so I'm beginning to think that I might be wasting my time."

"You are not wasting your time; you've just been misdirected. The word on the street is that your bandits are at it again."

Shocked, Sophie asked, "Are you serious?"

"Yes I am. The Eastern Shore Police Chiefs stick together, so here's the dip. The Deal Island Marina found a power boat adrift and a witness stated that two young men tried to sink it, but it wouldn't go down, the Marine Police stated that there were traces of cocaine onboard. Sound familiar?"

"It sure does, and it leads me to assume that this witness didn't see the boys leave."

"No, but a large motor launch was missing in the morning. The owner Tanner Bedford reported it to the Marine Police, and they haven't seen it yet."

"Tim thanks for the update and it sounds like I'm going to need to move north.

He said, "You need to remember that you be a woman alone on the Eastern Shore where they don't take to women telling them what to do. Make sure that you keep your wits about you at all times"

"I will and I'll call you at the end of the day to update you."

"I'll look for those calls."

<>

In the morning she had coffee with Tim, who had stayed in a room rather than take his motor

boat, home in the dark, after a couple of drinks they had the night before.

Before she left, Tim asked, "Sophie, please call of if you need me and add to that call at the end of each day to update me."

"I will."

They left and went separately to Crisfield; Tim went home on his boat and Sophie took the ferry to get her car.

It was a 42-minute drive to the Deal Island Marina. She parked on the lot and went in search of the owner or manager. She asked a man headed for the dock, "May I ask you for the name of the manager or owner and where I might find him or her?"

The man told her, "It's a man, his name is Thomas Lowe and his office, is in that small build on the other side of the parking lot."

"Thank you for your help."

The door was open, so tapped on it and with a gruff voice she heard, "What do you want? The slips are full."

She stepped into the office and said, "I'm not looking for a slip. My name is Sophie Brock and I work for the FBI in the Marine Forensic Crime Lab."

Lowe was tall and wiry and appeared to be about 60. Sophie knew immediately that he was gonna be a tough old bird for two reasons. The first was that she was an FBI Agent and the second and probably more important, she was a woman. She couldn't let him get in front of her case.

She pulled the photos from her bag and then asked, "Have you seen either of these young men?"

"Well miss, I gotta tell ya, I ain't looking for trouble with the F-B-I, so, a couple of scoundrels that match your photos showed up diesel for their boat and wanted to pay for it with cocaine."

"Mr. Lowe, that sounds like my bandits. Did you see which way they left?"

"No Miss, I did not but a trawler owned by Tanner Bedford was missing when I came in this morning. Let me grab a piece of paper and a pencil to write down the boat name with owner's phone number. Tell him that I gave you the number."

"Mr. Lowe, thank you for your help."

Even if he didn't trust western shore folks, the police, or women, he gave her a big lead. She walked to the Whitehaven Hotel and checked in. they had a rental she could use to drive to Arby's Dockside and Grill.

Before leaving for the restaurant, she called Tim, "It was a great day. Lowe gave me a couple of leads, so I'll check into them tomorrow. I haven't eaten since this morning, which means I need food and wine.

After disconnecting the call, Sophie drove to the Arby's Dockside and Grill, where she sat at the bar and ordered a cheeseburger with fries along with a glass of wine and returned to the White Haven Hotel where she fell semiconscious into the bed.

<>

Sophie rose early, showered, dressed, and then had breakfast before calling Tanner Bedford.

He answered on the first ring, "May I ask who's calling?"

"Yes of course you may. My name is Sophie Brock and I work for the FBI in the Marine Forensic Crime Lab. I'm in search of two young men who murdered a couple on their boat. These young men are also suspected for moving illegal drugs. I spoke with Thomas Lowe yesterday and he said that your boat was missing. Mr. Bedford has your boat been recovered yet?"

"Yes, it was towed to the Deal Island Marina earlier this morning."

"Mr. Bedford can you call Thomas Lowe and let him know we're on our way?"

Sophie wanted Tanner Bedford to know that she knew what was going on.

"Ms. Brock, I can do that."

"Before we disconnect the call, "I'm driving and so it should take me about 50 minutes to get there."

"That's not a problem. I'll have a fresh cup waiting for you when you get here."

"That would be great."

There was a delay on the bridge as they waited for the folks who worked off the island to move across it.

Tanner Bedford was waiting for her on the parking lot with two cups of hot coffee

Sophie thanked him as she took one of the cups. Bedford was a fine-looking man who appeared to be in his early 40's with curly brown hair. Sophie had to crane her neck way back to see his face, so it was her opinion that he was nearly 6'4" tall.

She could see that he was sizing her up as she introduced herself, "I'm Sophie Brock, we spoke yesterday about my gathering evidence. It's a pleasure to meet you face to face."

Bedford responded, "I agree, it's a pleasure to meet the person behind the voice on the phone. He went on to say that no one including him has been below on the boat.

Sophie said, "I'm glad to hear that. You can go below with me if you promise not to touch anything."

He responded with, "I promise."

She had her fingerprint kit in her bag along with the photos and names of her bandits.

As she handed the photos to Bedford she said, "This is who I am looking for."

He said, "I haven't seen anyone and didn't know my boat was missing until Tom called me."

He then stepped off the pier to his boat's deck and then put his hand out for Sophie to grab and step over to the boat.

Once she was securely on the boat, Tanner said, "This is the first time I've been on my boat since it was towed in,"

"Where did they find it?"

"I was told they found it adrift off the Black Water National Wildlife refuge."

"In that case let's get below to make sure that nothing was damaged. Tanner, I'd recommend having her hauled."

Nothing appeared to be damaged, so she pulled her kit from the bag and Tanner asked, "Are you looking for something specific now?"

"Yes, fingerprints, any sign of cocaine and whether or not there was an attempt to sink your boat. We know that it didn't sink because the Marine Police found it drifting, but double checking the situation can't hurt."

"Sophie, can I help?"

"Absolutely, working together, we'll get this done faster."

Sophie took fingerprints and put each one in an envelope and handed the envelope to Tanner to write the boat's name on it and then put them into her bag. Next were the vials for suspected cocaine.

She asked Tanner to look over the interior and check to make sure all the water locks were in place.

After he checked them, she said, "We're done and I don't about you, but I'm starving."

"In that case, let's get you to Arby's Dockside Bar and Grille."

While munching on cheeseburgers and fries, along with alcoholic beverages, Tanner asked, "Where are you staying"

She said, "The Whitehaven Inn. I hope to be gone early tomorrow to get the prints and traces of cocaine to the Crisfield Forensic Lab."

"Can you call me once you get the results?"

"Yes, I'll call you as soon as I get them."

<>

Sophie was up early, but before leaving for Crisfield, she called Tim to let him know that she was on her way to the Forensic Lab in Crisfield and that she had reservations to stay at the Tawesmore Inn.

She drove to Crisfield and checked into the Tawesmore Inn and then met Tim in the station's lobby. They took the new prints from Tanner Bedford's boat down to the forensic lab and then went to the Waterman's Inn for dinner.

During dinner, Sophie updated Tim about her time on Deal Island. She said, "We went below and to see if there was any water coming in and there wasn't, so I took fingerprints and Tanner bagged them. My boys are apparently learning about transporting drugs because there was nothing in the cabin like there was on the Jolly Roger."

Tim drove them back to the station and before they reached the station, "Sophie, if the prints are a match, what's your next step?"

"If they match, I have to get the word out about these two drug runners."

They made their way down to the Forensic Lab to find a match to her young bandits. She was excited, but the matches meant she had to work harder to find this two little drug dealers, wondering what their parents would say, when she got them in jail.

She broke away from her thoughts to tell Tim, "I'm so tired that I can't see or think straight, so can we meet in the morning for coffee and then you can help me figure out what to do next."

She was so tired that she drove like an old woman to the Inn. Once she made her way to her room, Sophie calls Tanner. He answered on the first ring and asked, "Did you learn anything useful from the lab."

"Yes, the prints matched, but there was no trace of cocaine, which means to me that they might be get smarter on the transfer or they got caught sneaking some for the drugs by the person they're working for."

"Sophie, thank you for calling with the lab results, you sound tired, so get some rest and we'll talk later."

"That works for me."

After disconnecting the call, she was so tired that she went to the bed where she slept soundly until morning.

<>

Sophie woke in the morning feeling great after a good night of restful sleep. She showered, dressed, and then went down to have coffee with Tim. She sat across from him at a table for two, and smiled as she said, "Good Morning."

"Good Morning to you as well, were you able to get hold of the guy with the boat you inspected?"

"I called him last night to let him know the lab results."

"What did he say?"

"Tim, is this an interrogation? He said to call if I needed his help."

"Sophie, are you planning to call him?"

"Yes, if I can use his help and at this point, I may need all an all-hands on deck alert."

Tim asked, "What's on your dance card today?

"Before I do anything, I need to make a list of agency alerts."

Tim asked, "Like whom?"

"I need to call the Marine Police, the Drug Enforcement Agency and of course my boss at the Federal Bureau of Investigation."

"How long will that take?"

"It shouldn't take long."

"Okay, what do you do after the calls are made?"

"Wait until someone calls me."

"Sophie, I have to say that sounds like a boring day to me."

"I certainly don't want you to endure a boring day, so do you have any suggestions?"

"I do, you have a cell phone that the other agencies will call, so we'll do a little sightseeing of Crisfield."

"Are you serious?"

"Yes, I am, because in my opinion you need to take a break and clear your head and walking through Crisfield might help."

He drove them to the Janes Island Park where he told Sophie, "Take your shoes off and leave them in the car."

Sophie wasn't sure if she wanted to do that, but she went ahead and took them off and followed Tim onto the beach in the warm sunshine along with a cool breeze. She walked down to the water's edge where she rolled her pants up to get her toes into the cold water. The tension in her body disappeared, causing her to say, "Tim, this is what I needed. Thank you for bringing me here."

Tim asked, "Are you up for some lunch?"

"I'm starving."

"Will the Bubba Wing Shack work?"

"It sure will."

They sat at the bar and Tim ordered their lunch and while munching on wings with wine, Sophie said, "Tim, I can't thank you enough for getting me out of my room to enjoy a great morning on the beach in the warm sunshine and the cool breeze."

"Sophie, I'd hoped to get out of the room and into the sunshine, which you would relax."

"Well it worked."

"I'm going to drive you to the Inn and come for you at 7:00 to take you to dinner at the Waterman's Inn."

Sophie napped until Tim called to say, "I'm on my way to pick you up."

They sat at the bar for dinner, the drinks arrived first and then Tim ordered their dinners.

During dinner Tim asked, "Sophie, what's your role when someone calls?"

"Well, I called the agencies, so it's likely that I'll get the call. If the Marine Police calls and ask me what they should do. I'll need to ask a few questions, such as if drugs were found, and if they were, I'll call the DEA and if someone is found dead, that call is mine to investigate.

"What will you do until then?"

"Stay close to the hotel, so I can get to wherever fast."

Tim drove her back to the hotel and asked, "Sophie, please call and let me know whether or not you received a call."

As Sophie got out of the car she said, "Thank you again for a great day and I promise to call you in the morning to have coffee with me."

She went to bed and slept soundly until morning.

<>

She showered, dressed, and went down for breakfast and found Tim in the lobby drinking a cup of coffee, so she asked, "Tim, have you had breakfast yet?"

"No, I haven't."

"In that case, come with me to have breakfast."

The breakfast foods were set up on a buffet, so they each grabbed a plate and filled it with breakfast goodies and found a table for two to sit at.

Once they were seated, Tim asked, "Have you heard from anyone yet, about your bandits?"

"Not a word, so I'm beginning to wonder where they are?"

He didn't want to upset her by telling her that they've had enough time to run to Canada or Mexico to lay low.

As if she read his mind, Sophie said, "I just hope they're still somewhere along the Bay dealing drugs and not killing people to do it."

"I can't agree more. Do you want to do something today, so you don't lose your mind?"

"Tim thanks for the offer, but my gut is telling me that a call is coming today."

Even though, he didn't believe her gut could tell her anything, he said, "Please call me when it does."

"I will definitely call you as soon as it does."

Tim left to drive to the station thinking about Sophie's gut feeling.

After Tim left, Sophie wondered if in fact her gut was going to let her down. She spent the rest of the morning fretting about it. Going out for a walk did help so she decided to watch the news in her room. When that didn't distract her from worrying, she went down to the Inn's library to find a book to take to her room to read. She'd just settled in to read and damn if her cell phone didn't ring. She was sure that it was Tim, but the CID was wrong, so she answered it with, "May I ask whose calling?"

"My name is Jon Harris and I'm a Marine Police Officer and I'm calling to let you know that your bandits are in the Chesterfield Jail."

"How did you find them?"

"They were transferring drugs from one boat to a larger one and as we watched to make sure they were the bandits you put out the alert for."

"Mr. Harris, have you contacted the Drug Enforcement Administration yet?"

"Yes, and they're on their way here."

"So am I after I made a phone call."

She called Tim, "I'm on my way to Chesterfield where my bandits are in jail"

"When did you get the call?"

"Not long after you left a Marine Police officer called to say his team watched them transfer drugs from one boat to another one and called both me and the DEA, so I'll call you when I get back."

She then started her two-and-a-half-hour journey to the Chestertown Police Department stopping once refuel and grab a cup of coffee; arriving in just under three-hours, so she went into the station to announce herself to the Police Chief, Andrew Packard who appeared to be a rather short man, standing at 5'11"with grey eyes and grey short cropped hair.

"Chief Packard, my name is Sophie Brock and I'm an FBI Agent and I work in the Forensic Crime Lab."

He put his hand out to shake hers as he hers as he said, "It's a pleasure to meet you Agent Brock. I have to say that I've not seen this much hustle and bustle since we launched *The Sultana* launched in 2001."

Drug Enforcement Agent Nicole Hensley, who stood 5'7" tall with bobbed brown hair that matched her light brown eyes, was standing off to one side waiting for Sophie to finish with her introduction to the Chief.

She walked over and asked, "Sophie, it's been a long time since we've seen one another."

As they hugged one another, Sophie said, "It sure has."

Nicole asked, "What brings you here?"

"The two noticeably young bandits in the cell are responsible for the murder of two folks on their boat. I also found traces of cocaine on the galley counter, so I made sure that DEA got the word."

Chief Packard, interrupted their conversation to ask, "Who is going into the Interview Room First?"

Sophie went first since she had them on Murder charges, she brought George Patrick into the inter room first and identified herself to him, "Mr. Patrick, my name is Sophie Brock and I work for the FBI in the Marine Forensic Lab. Your fingerprints along with traces of cocaine were found in the cabin of the Jolly Rogers along with the dead bodies of Skye and Malcom Stanford."

She asked, "Why did you and Harold murder the two folks who owned the boat?"

"Our boss told us to murder them before we left the boat."

"I'll go for that. Please tell me your boss's name"

"I'm not at liberty to say."

"That is your choice; however, I'm going to charge you with murder and that means you'll spend the rest of your life in a prison cell."

As she walked him back to his cell, she thought he was just too young to give up his life for someone who he was not at liberty to give his name and hoped Simms would be more cooperative.

She walked him to the interview room and told him to sit while she introduced herself, "Mr. Simms, my name is Sophie Brock and I work for the FBI in the Marine Forensic Lab. The two of you will be charged with the murder with the death of Skye and Malcom Stanford. I talked with your buddy George Patrick, and he has chosen to spend his life in prison rather than give up your boss's name."

"In that case, I hope to the cell either next to him or across from him."

Nicole was in the hall and as she and Sophie passed, she asked, "How did it go?

"They're willing to spend the rest of their life in prison before giving up their boss's name."

"Thanks for sharing that, but I don't expect to get any more than you did."

She interviewed them in the same order, so George Patrick went first, "Mr. Patrick, my name is Nicole Hensley and I work for the Drug Enforcement Agency and I'd like to ask you a few questions."

"You and Harold Simms were caught red-handed transferring drugs from one boat to another by the Marine Police. If you give me the name of your boss I might able to as the US Attorney to lenient sentence due to your age."

"You don't get, Harold and I are already the walking dead because he knows everything we do or say."

"If that's true and you are already dead, giving me his name now won't make you any less dead and if we get to him, before he gets to you, we'll have the opportunity to take him to jail for life and you Harold will be eligible for the Witness Protection Program."

"You really don't get it, so I'm gonna keep my mouth shut."

Nicole walked Patrick back to the cell and pulled Harold Simms out; Harold appeared to be the brighter one of the two.

She walked him to the interview room and introduced herself, "My name is Nicole Hensley and I an Agent with the Drug Enforcement Agency. You and your partner, George Patrick were caught red-handed transferring drugs from one boat to another by the Marine Police. Do you have a legitimate explanation?"

"Agent Hensley, I might not be able to give you an explanation, because our package wasn't delivered and that means we're both the walking dead."

"Why is that?"

"The man we work for doesn't like late or no deliveries."

Hensley asked, "Is there a reason why?"

"Yes, he said he's on a schedule so when we're late he gets angry and threatens to kill us."

"Harold, you and George are so young, so what led to work for this guy?"

"We were homeless drug addicts who bought from someone he knew; we owed the dealer a lot of money. He said that we could pay off the debt and then money if we worked for his boss."

"Did you get paid well?"

"At first, but once we paid off our dealer, we were just mules to move his drugs for him. We always grabbed some of his cocaine, to sell on the side."

"Harold, I know that you're not going to give me his name, but let me say, he has no right to threaten your life and make you his drug dealing mule. I'm going to give you my card and if you change your mind about giving up his name, call me."

She walked him back to the cell and asked, "Sophie, are you up for some food along with an alcoholic beverage?"

"I sure am, so lead on."

They jumped into Nicole's car and she drove them to O'Connor's Pub and Restaurant and sat at the bar. They ordered their beverages first and when they came, they cheeseburgers with fries,

Nicole asked, "How long have you worked for the FBI?"

"Let me think, about six years."

"Did you ever get married?"

"Nope, how about you, did you ever get married?"

"No, because I couldn't find a guy who thought I was a DEA agent to prove that I was better than the male agents. Sophie, I need to talk business for a moment. Your murder charges take president over my drug charges."

"In that case, I'll ask the judge in Crisfield tomorrow for warrants. Do you know where the US District Court is?"

"The closest US District Court is in Baltimore."

They checked into the White Swann Bed and Breakfast to spend the night.

Chapter Three

Nicole and Sophie had breakfast together in the White Swan Inn, where Nicole asked, "Since the bandits are going to Crisfield first, would you mind if I followed you to watch the trial?"

"Of course not, and If I can, I'll join you in Baltimore to see what happens to them in the federal court."

Before leaving for Crisfield, Sophie called Tim, "I'm on my way to Crisfield and have a DEA Agent following me."

It was a two-and-a-half-hour drive before they parked on the police station lot. They walked through the front door chatting about how easy the drive had been when, Sophie saw that Tim was waiting for them, so Sophie made the introductions, "Tim Willoughby, is Crisfield's Chief of Police. Tim this is agent Nicole Hensley of the Drug Enforcement Agency. She plans to stay for the trial and then they become her bandits to transport to the US District Court charged with Drug Trafficking."

They shook hands and both said it's a pleasure to meet you and then Tim asked, "Sophie, where are your two bandits"

"Somewhere behind us, the State Police are bringing them. I wanted to call an Assistant State Attorney to read the Miranda rights to them."

"In that case, go into my office and call Alfred Pearson."

She placed the call and when he answered, she said, "My name is Sophie Brock, I'm an FBI Agent in the Marine Criminal Forensic Lab. I took two noticeably young men into custody for First Degree Murder. I have not yet Mirandized them. "

"Ms. Brock, please call me when they arrive, and I'll come to the station to read the Miranda Rights to them and then see what we have."

"I can to that."

Sophie left Tim's Office to update them on what the Assistant State's Attorney told her. She then had another cup of coffee while they waited.

Her bandits were delivered before she finished her coffee by two Maryland State Police Officers, as she signed the form that she'd taken custody of them, Tim put them in the cell.

Sophie made the call to Alfred Pearson, "Mr. Pearson, this is Sophie Brock; my two bandits are in the Crisfield Jail."

"Ms. Brock, what are you planning to charge them with?"

She said, "First Degree Murder."

"If I remember correctly, you have not read them their Miranda Rights?"

"Mr. Pearson, you are correct, I have not read them their Miranda Rights, but I have evidence as proof of their murder."

"I'm on my way to the station."

Pearson entered the Police Station and asked for Sophie Brock

He was a lean young man dressed in a fine-looking suit. He had blonde curly hair and blue eyes

She stepped forward from the group she was standing with, "I'm Sophie Brock."

Pearson put his hand out to shake hers, as he said, "It's a pleasure to meet you Ms. Brock, you have quite a reputation on the Bay."

She chuckled and then said, "I hope that it's a good one."

"It most certainly is. You said on the phone call that you had evidence to share with me, so why don't we go into the interview room so I can look it over."

Sophie sat quietly as he read Joseph Clifford's report.

"This report states that these two folks died by drowning and not the knife wounds."

"Mr. Pearson, I was as shocked as you are now. Her parents aren't aware of what they died from; however, I'll have to tell them once a trial date has been set."

"Ms. Brock, I'm planning to get these two into court as quickly as I can, so please call them as quickly as you can."

"What do you mean by as quickly as you can? Her parents live on the Western Shore. Are you suggesting that I call them today?"

"Yes, that's what I'm suggesting."

"Let's finish the interviews before you call them. Please bring your first bandit to the interview room."

Sophie brought George Patrick to the interview room.

Pearson introduced himself, "My name is Alfred Pearson. I'm the prosecutor in this case. May I ask you for your name?"

"Sure, it's George Patrick."

"Mr. Patrick, I'm going to read you your Miranda Rights. He read them to Patrick and then asked if he understood them."

"Yes, sir I do."

"Then please sign this form, confirming that you understand your rights."

Without issue, Patrick signed the form.

"Mr. Patrick, do you know why you've been charged with Murder?"

"Yes, sir, I do. We should have thrown them overboard and let them drown in the water."

"Mr. Patrick please stay seated while I get a Public Defender to come here and give you a decent defense."

He stepped out of the interview room to ask if there was a phone he could use.

Tim said, "Yes there's one in my office, just follow me."

Pearson called Public Defender Jacob Beacham and asked, "Jacob, do you had time to defend a person for the charge of Murder?"

"Alfred, are you at the Police Department?"

"Yes, meet me in the interview room."

He left Tim's office to tell Agent Brock, "I just called a public defendant to represent George Patrick, so why don't you return him to his cell while we wait and bring Harold Simms into the interview room."

Sophie put George Patrick into the cell and pulled Harold Simms out to walk to the interview room.

Simms sat across from Pearson, who introduced himself, "My name is Alfred Pearson and I'm the Prosecutor for this case. I want to you listen as I read you your Miranda Rights and if you understand them, please sign the form."

"Mr. Pearson, I understand them." He signed the form and slid it across the table to Pearson.

Before Pearson said a word, Simms said, "I'm entitled to lawyer and I'll talk once I have one"

Pearson left the Interview Room to let Agent Brock know that Simms told him that he'll talk once he has an attorney.

"In that case let me get him back in the cell. Would you like a cup of coffee?"

"Thank you because I would."

Everyone sat in the police station's lobby drinking coffee while waiting for Public Defender Jacob Beacham.

Pearson casually said, "I still need to get a warrant from Judge Adam Myers, before formally arresting them."

Defense Attorney Jacob Beacham entered the station front door looking a bit surprised by the number of people in the lobby area, so Tim made the introductions and offered him a cup of coffee.

"Thanks for the offer, but I've too much already today."

Pearson and Beacham spoke quietly together before he asked Agent Brock to bring George Patrick to the interview room.

They entered the room together and Pearson left after Beacham introduced himself to George Patrick.

"Mr. Patrick, my name is Jacob Beacham and I will be your defense attorney. In your own words, please tell me why you were taken into custody."

"Yes sir, I can do that. We should have thrown them overboard, so they could drown in the water."

"Mr. Patrick, throw who overboard?"

"The couple on the boat that we were putting a load of cocaine on and move it to Smith Island for a hand off to another boat."

"Mr. Patrick, "Can you tell me if you work for someone who told you that you should throw the victims overboard?"

"Yes sir, I do."

"Mr. Patrick, can you tell me the person's name?"

"No sir, I cannot."

"Is there a reason that you cannot tell me the person's name?"

"Yes sir, there is, Harold told me that if I gave his name, that the person would kill us both."

"I won't ask for his name anymore but is it the same person who told you where to bring the drugs and how to transfer them."

"Yes sir, it is."

"Thank you, Mr. Patrick. I believe that I have everything that I need to give you a good defense."

Agent Brock walked Patrick back to the cell and waited for Pearson to ask for Simms.

Before asking Agent Brock to bring Simms to the interview room, he introduced himself to DEA Agent Nicole Hensley.

"Ms. Hensley, my name is Alfred Pearson and I work as an Assistant State's Attorney. I've only interviewed one of the suspected murders yet, but I believe they were working for a major drug dealer, so if either of them gives me something, I'll make sure that I pass it on to you."

Nicole managed to keep her sarcasm under control as she graciously said, "Thank you Mr. Pearson for your help."

"Agent Brock, we're ready for Harold Simms."

Sophie passed Nicole in the hall and listened as she said, "Pearson's trying to tell me how to do my job."

"We'll talk over dinner."

Sophie pulled Harold Simms from the cell, as she walked him to the interview room; she was thinking he was smarter than Patrick as she wondered how it would go in the interview room.

The two lawyers followed her to the interview room.

"Mr. Simms, while you know me, I want to introduce you to Jacob Beacham, who will serve as your defense attorney. I'm gonna leave the room so the two of you can speak privately."

Beacham said, "Mr. Simms, I'm going to tell you that without telling me the truth, I won't be able to give you a good defense."

Simms sat silently, not even acknowledging that Beacham was in the room with him.

"If you're not going to talk with me, I'm going to wish you luck in the courtroom."

Beacham left the interview room and told Pearson, "That young man is gonna spend the rest of his life in jail. He wouldn't say a word to me which means I can't defend him. I'll stand with him when he's asked to stand, but he gave me nothing that I could work with to provide him a defense strategy."

As the two attorneys left the station, Pearson said, "In the morning, I'll ask the Judge for arrest warrant and that might shake him up enough to talk."

<>

After the attorneys left, Tim made sure for the night and then asked, "Where would you two ladies like to have dinner?"

Sophie quickly said, "The Watermen's Inn. Are you planning to feed the kids?"

"Yes, I am, my evening dispatcher will be in soon and take care of feeding them."

Tim drove them to the restaurant and was delighted when he was able to secure a table, because this restaurant fills to capacity with diners.

Once they were seated, Tim asked, "What beverage should I order for the two of you?"

They both said in stereo, "Cabernet", so he ordered a bottle for them and a Heineken draft for him.

Sophie and Nicole picked out the appetizers and the entrees for all three to share.

Sophie asked, "Nicole what did you want to talk about?"

"Alfred Pearson stopped me in the hall and tried to tell me how to do my job."

Tim said, "Nicole, please don't take personally because he does that to everyone. He tried to tell me that in order to be a good chief that I had to make more arrests. He didn't care for what or who I arrested; he just thought I should increase the numbers."

"Well I think that he should stick to what he does for a living and leave us to do ours."

After that topic was off the table, the conversation moved on to lighter topics, sports, travel places and of course, how many years were left to work before retiring.

Sophie paid the dinner tab and Tim drove them to the station where their cars were parked.

Nicole then followed Sophie to the Tawesmore Inn.

Sophie took a minute to call Helen and Fred Barton to let them know that the bandits were in custody and had a chance of being in the Crisfield Courthouse tomorrow

Both were tired to there wasn't any conversation as they went to their respective room.

Chapter Four

Tim joined Sophie and Nicole for a quiet breakfast. Everyone was wondering what today would be like, and how it would play out with the bandits.

Tim said, "I'll put my money down that they'll at least be in court for an arraignment."

Sophie said, "That might be true, but if there's a jury trial there might be an arraignment and then we'll bring them back to the jail and wait."

Nicole added, "Sophie, that's been my experience, but I've never been involve in a case on the Eastern Shore."

Tim said, "I've been to a few trials here on the Eastern Shore and Judge Adams Meyers tends to run his courtroom by the mood he's in. Ladies if you want to be there before the attorneys, we gotta go now." He drove them to the station where their cars and the bandits were. He checked in with his dispatcher and was told that the guys in the cell were fed this morning.

Alfred and Pearson arrived together.

Pearson said, "Judge Adam Myers is putting a jury together while we issue the warrants which are in my briefcase. Agent Brock, please bring them in one at a time so I can issue the warrants individually."

Sophie brought George Patrick to the interview and when Pearson formally arrest him, the kid started to cry saying over and over that he only did what he was told what to do.

Pearson was surprised that the crying him hard in the chest for this young boy, but Patrick was involved in murder and that was his own doing.

Pearson left the interview room and asked Agent Brock, "Please return Patrick to the cell and bring me Harold Simms."

Simms was without emotion when Pearson formally arrested him. He wouldn't look at Pearson or acknowledge his existence. He figured if Simms wouldn't talk, he wasn't gonna push it.

Pearson left the interview room to tell Agent Brock to put him back into the cell when his phone rang.

Judge Myers was on the phone, "Counselor, we're ready, so bring them to the Courthouse."

Tim drove the bandits to the courthouse using his patrol car. Sophie and Nicole followed him using Nicole's car.

Tim handed the two bandits over to the Court Marshall, who would put them in the Courthouse jail.

The Barton's were standing in the hallway looking as though they weren't sure where they should be.

Sophie went over and introduced herself and said she was sorry for their loss. She took in a deep breath to get her courage up to tell them about the Medical Examiner's Report.

That sent them into a round of hard crying.

Sophie asked Tim, "The Barton's aren't looking good, can you get them settled in the courtroom."

"I sure can."

He walked to where they were standing and introduced himself, "My name is Tim Willoughby and I'm the Chief of Police for Crisfield. I'm not going to be called as a witness which means that I have the opportunity to sit with you for the entire trial."

"Chief, we are the parents of Skye and her husband, Malcom. My name is Fred, and this is my wife, Helen. We both appreciate that you will stay with us throughout the trial."

Nicole had followed Tim into the courtroom and sat beside him. She leaned over him to introduce herself, "My name is Nicole Hensley and I'm a Drug Enforcement Agent and after this trial, I'll be sending them to the US District Court in Baltimore, MD for drug charges."

Helen asked, "Will we be able to watch the trial?"

"Of course, you can."

She handed Mrs. Barton two of her cards and said, "Write your name and number on one of the cards, and give it to me, so I can call you with the dates when I know them."

Helen thanked her just before Albert Pearson entered the courtroom and walked to the State's Table and sat.

Fred whispered to Tim, "Is that the prosecutor for this case?"

Tim whispered back, "Yes he is."

Jacob Beacham and his two defendants were next, George Patrick and Harold Simms walked to the defense table and all three sat.

Helen gasped, "They're just babies."

Tim leaned over to say, "Remember they are being charged with First Degree Murder."

"I know, but in my opinion, they're still babies."

The Bailiff entered the court to call out, "Hear Ye, Hear Ye, all stand as the Honorable Adams Meyers enters the courtroom, for Case Number 17-053, for Murder in the First Degree in Violation of Maryland Criminal Code §201by one George Patrick and one Harold Simms."

Once Judge Meyers was seated on the bench, he said, "Everyone may take a seat."

He then went on to ask, "Will the defendants please stand"

Beacham stood with Patrick and Simms, as the Judge asked how they pled.

Patrick waited for Simms to say. "Not Guilty."

Then he followed with "Not Guilty."

Judge Meyers said, "You may sit."

Judge Meyers asked, "Will the State move forward with its Probable Cause."

"Thank You, Your Honor."

"The State has evidence to show that the defendants stabbed the victim's multiple times; however, the cause of death was drowning in the cabin of their sailboat, *The Jolly Roger*. The State has evidence to show that the defendants' fingerprints were found in the boat's cabin and matched the defendants' NCIC Report."

"Thank you, counselor, I believe that we'll move on to Opening Summaries unless there's a need for a break. Is there anyone in the courtroom needing a break?"

When there was none, Judge Meyers asked the State to proceed with its Opening Summary

Pearson stood and walked toward the jury; then turned to walk toward the defense table, knowing that all eyes were on him, including Judge Meyers. Now that he had everyone's attention, he spoke, "Don't let the defendants' young appearance lead you away from what they did. The two defendants were unmerciful when they first stabbed Helen and Fred Barton. Then to make sure they finished the job by laying them down face first in the boat's incoming water to drown. I will present evidence and witness testimony to ensure there is no doubt for a verdict of guilty."

"Thank you, Your Honor, the State has concluded its Opening Summery."

Everyone in the courtroom heard Helen Barton's cry of dismay.

Fred held his wife tightly as he tried to sooth her.

While he couldn't stop the process, Judge Meyers' heart went out to her. "Is the Defense ready to present its Opening Summary?"

"Yes, Your Honor, it is ready."

Beacham walked toward the jury and like Pearson, turned and walked toward the defense table and like Pearson, every eye in the courtroom was on him waiting to hear what he would say. "You heard the State say, not to let the *defendants' young appearance lead you away from what they did.* I'm going to challenge that statement. They *are* incredibly young and not knowledgeable as to how the judicial system works. It would serve no purpose to imprison them for the rest of their lives. I'm going to urge the jury to acquit these two young boys so that they will go forward and learn from their behavior."

"Thank you, Your Honor, the Defense has concluded its Opening Summary"

As he walked to the defense table, he hoped that he left some room for doubt.

Judge Meyers announced, "I believe that a fifteen-minute break is in order before moving on to witness testimony"

During the break, Fred walked with wife to the restroom and told her, "Helen, please wipe the tears from your face, because we still have a long way to go."

She came out of the Ladies restroom looking better. They made their way back into the courtroom, to listen to witness testimony.

When everyone returned to the courtroom, Judge Meyer asked the State to call its first witness to the stand.

Pearson called for Steven Clark to take the stand.

Pearson waited until the bailiff swore Steven Clark in.

Pearson then approached the witness and asked, "Please state your name for the record."

"Steven Thomas Clark"

"Mr. Clark, are you employed?"

"Yes I am. I'm a Medical Examiner in Crisfield, Maryland."

Pearson handed him the report and asked him, "Mr. Clark, is this your report?"

"Yes sir, it is."

"Mr. Clark, will you please read the highlighted text in this report."

Clark read it aloud, so everyone could hear, "The victims had been stabbed multiple times; however, they were placed face down and drowned in their own blood along with the incoming water from the open scuppers in the boat's cabin."

A horrifying scream went up in the courtroom and Helen Barton ran out of the courtroom.

Judge Meyers asked, "Is that woman okay?"

Tim stood to explain what happened, "Your Honor that was the victim's mother, Helen Barton. Agent Hensley followed her out."

"Thank you, Chief Willoughby, please keep me apprised of the situation."

"I will Your Honor."

Judge Meyers asked Beacham, "Counselor would you like to cross this witness?"

"No, Your Honor, I would not."

The Judge then said, "Mr. Clark, you may step down"

He then asked, "Does the state have another witness to call?"

"Yes, Your Honor, it does, the State would like to call Sophie Brock to the stand."

While she walked to the witness stand, she thought that while she had testified in a number of cases, none hit her as hard as when she saw Helen Barton leaves the courtroom, screaming."

The Bailiff came into the hall and said, "You're up next, so follow me in and I'll swear you in"

After she was sworn in, Pearson asked her to state her full name for the record.

Everyone in the courtroom could see the strain on her face as she answered, "Sophie Margaret Brock."

Pearson asked, "Ms. Brock, are you employed and if so, where?

"I work for the Federal Bureau of Investigation in the Marine Crime Forensic Lab unit."

Pearson smiled as he asked. "May I present you with the report you wrote and ask that you read the highlighted text?"

"Fingerprints from the interior of the boat's cabin matched the fingerprints run through NCIC for George Patrick and Harold

Simms. Traces of cocaine were bagged for the Drug Enforcement Agency."

Judge Meyers thanked her for her concise testimony and then asked if Beacham wanted to cross?

"No, Your Honor, I do not wish to cross?"

Judge Meyers said, "Agent Brock, you may step down."

Judge Meyers said, "We'll take a short break before we hear the Defense's Closing Summary."

When everyone returned from the break, the Bailiff called for everyone to stand as the Honorable Adam Meyers enters the courtroom.

Judge Meyers said, "Please be seated. The defense may proceed with its Closing Summation."

Beacham stood to say, "Thank you, Your Honor." He then made his way to the jury box, he then held his hand out to say, "What you see sitting at the defense table are two young boys, who may have been led astray by someone who they will not say for fear of being murdered. Do not judge them as murderers, but as two young men, boys really, who traveled down the wrong path. If you believe that to be true, you must acquit them."

Beacham went to sit at the defense table.

Pearson said, "Thank you, Your Honor." He walked to the defense table and said, "The defense attorney told you that these were two young boys, who traveled down the wrong path. Let me assure you that these two young men chose their path and that included murdering Helen and Frederick Barton without emotion or remorse. Don't let them hide behind someone else who they say would murder them. Focus on the victims, who had no say in the situation. These two young men committed a heinous crime of murder and if you agree, you must return with a guilty verdict."

Agent Hensley asked Tim, "What did we miss?"

"The Closing Summaries for both the prosecutor and the defense."

"Tim, in your opinion, how did it go?"

"Nicole, I'm not sure I have an opinion to share, the State pushed for guilty and the defense pushed for acquittal, quite normal."

"I understand, so I guess we need to wait for the jury's verdict."

Judge Meyers asked that Bailiff to walk the jury to the jury room

Judge Meyers follow the jury into the room to give them the rules to decide the verdict.

"First, the members of the jury will choose one member to represent them as a foreman or forewoman. It is that person and only that person who will send questions to me through the bailiff. Second, this is a capital offense, so there're must be a unanimous vote for either guilty or innocent. Before I leave, are there any questions?"

There were none, so Judge Meyers left the jury room to announce from the Bench, "The jury is now deliberating, so it might be a good time, to take a break and get something to eat. The defendants were taken to the Court lockup, where they will be fed."

Pearson and Beacham left the courtroom, to get some lunch.

No one in Sophie's group made a move. It was a tense wait and everyone remained silent. One by one they left to use the restroom, but most of the time, they remained seated.

Helen was quietly crying, so Fred held onto her tightly to hold off his own tears.

The Bailiff entered the courtroom with Pearson, Beacham along with Patrick and Simms in tow. Once they were seated, he left the courtroom, to bring the jury in and once they were seated, he left the courtroom and shortly to call out for everyone to stand as The Honorable Adam enters the courtroom.

Sophie's group sat tall, looking nervous because they knew that this was it.

Judge Meyers asked, "Has the jury reached a verdict?"

The foreman stepped for to say, "We have Your Honor."

The foreman handed the paper that contained the verdict to the bailiff who in turn handed it to Judge Meyers who looked at it and returned it to the bailiff, who walked it to the foreman.

Judge Meyer asked for the Jury's verdict.

The foreman stated that they had unanimously voted guilty for the charge of First-Degree Murder.

Since this was a capital offense, Judge Meyers polled each member of the jury to hear how they voted and if they had been coerced to cast a vote for guilty?

All twelve members said they had not been coerced into the plea of guilty.

Judge Meyers said, "I want to thank the jury for doing its civic duty. The Bailiff will walk you to the Clerk's Office where your checks are."

Once the Jury left the courtroom, Judge Meyers asked the defendants to step forward and asked if they had anything to say?

George Patrick cried, and Harold Simms just stood stoically.

Judge Meyers sentenced them to life sentences without the benefit of Parole.

Judge Meyers told Agent Hensley that two Deputy US Marshals were on standby to transport Patrick and Simms to the Baltimore City Jail.

Helen and Fred along with Nicole, Sophie and Tim went to dinner at the Watermen Inn to celebrate the verdict.

Helen said, "While I'm glad they were convicted for murdering my daughter and her husband, I'm not sure how to say this, but they both threw away their lives. They'll never get married or have children and I can't help but think that's sad."

The table was quiet for a moment while everyone absorbed what Helen said, because it was so true.

Fred said, "Helen, while I understand what you're saying, those two boys are alive, Skye and Malcom are not, so I can't feel sorry for them."

"You're right Fred, so I have to get my head in the right place to remember that they maliciously murdered our children. Okay everyone, we need to do some celebrating tonight."

The atmosphere lightened as well as the conversation just delighting in one another's company.

Tim said, "I sure am going to miss everyone when you leave for Baltimore."

Sophie told him, "I promise to call you."

After eating and drinking their fill, Sophie paid the tab and Helen and Fred, along with Sophie and Nicole made their way to the Tawesmore Inn. They had long drives, tomorrow, so they went to bed.

Chapter Five

Tim joined them for breakfast at the Tawesmore Inn and when it was time to leave, he gave everyone a hug goodbye and watched as they pulled out to caravan their way to the Western Shore. He was gonna miss them; because, Crisfield hadn't seen that much excitement since the 2012 murder that shook the town for months.

Before leaving for the Western Shore, Nicole suggested they use a code for pulling over, flash your high beams. She took the lead for the 3 ½ hour drive. Traffic was light and even with the two stops they made, they made good time.

They separated on I-695 to drive to their respective homes.

Sophie grabbed a shower and glass of wind before calling Tim to tell him, "We're home."

"How was the drive?'

"Traffic was light, so it was an easy drive home."

<>

Nicole called the Baltimore City Jail to confirm that Patrick and Simms were there. The duty officer said they were there and because of their young age they were in separate solitary confinement cells.

That satisfied her worry about them getting murdered before testifying, so she went to bed.

<>

In the morning, Nicole showered and dressed, she then completed her trip report over a cup of coffee. She then called Assistant US Attorney Stacey Greenwood. They had worked together on a number of cases.

When she answered the phone, Nicole updated Greenwood with what she had, "I have two very cantankerous young men who were caught red-handed transferring cocaine from one boat to another by Jon Harris of the Marine Police. I have his signed report to show you."

"Nicole, will he testify in Court to support his report?"

"Yes, he will."

"Have you mirandized the two defendants yet?

"No, I have not."

"That's not a problem, let's meet at the jail and Mirandized them and then I'll get the arrest warrant from Judge Adam Hammond. Do you know if they need defense counsel?"

"Yes, they do."

"Let me call Federal Public Defender Patricia Atkins to let her know that she has work coming her way. Once I have the warrants and execute them, Hammond's gonna want to arraign them as quickly as possible, so you need to be ready for that."

"I understand and will be ready."

They drove separately to the Baltimore City Correctional Center. Greenwood signed in the log first and Hensley signed in behind her. Greenwood had requested that Patrick and Simms be brought together to the interview room.

Greenwood and Hensley entered to interview room and both defendants were sitting at the table.

Greenwood read them their Miranda Rights and asked if they understood them, they both nodded their head, so Greenwood asked, "Please sign your name on this form to acknowledge that you were read your Miranda Rights and understand them." She slid a form across the table to each defendant.

She noticed that Patrick could barely sign his name. Greenwood put both forms to the side and asked Patrick first, "Do you know why you are in jail."

He responded, "I'm not sure."

Greenwood asked Simms the same question and he said, "Drug Trafficking, George and I are the walking because we were taken into custody before the drugs were delivered."

Patrick said, "I remember now, some guy took us in custody before we delivered the drugs and the rest is what Harold said."

Greenwood told them, "The jail guards will put you back in your cell and I'll be back tomorrow to formally arrest you."

Greenwood waited until the guards removed George Patrick and Harold Simms from the interview room, before suggesting that they go and get some lunch.

Nicole followed Stacy to Momma Mias. They sat at the bar where they both ordered wine and cheeseburgers with French fries.

While they were eating, Stacy said, "I'm not quite sure how to handle Patrick. He could barely write, and he repeated what Simms said."

"That's how he behaved in Crisfield for the murder charge."

Stacey said, "Well, that shows that he's a follower and not a leader, so in my opinion that's sad. I've never in my career, worried about how the defendant felt; this is a first for me."

Nicole understood how sad it was for Stacey because she felt the same way during the murder trial in Crisfield.

Nicole asked, "Is it too soon to call Officer Matt Harris?"

"No, it's not, but I'll call him when I get home."

Nicole paid the tab and they left.

Stacy called Matt Harris, to let him know that Patrick and Simms might be arraigned tomorrow in the US District Court.

"I plan to come over tonight and stay with a friend."

Nicole then called Sophie, to let her know that the arraignment might be tomorrow, she said, "I'll call the Barton's and let them know."

Fred asked, "What time should Helen and I get to the courthouse?"

Sophie knew how expensive downtown parking was, so she suggested, "Why don't I pick you up at 7:00 and we'll have breakfast in Jimmy's in Fell's Point before we go to the courthouse."

"We'll be ready. Sophie will you be testifying?"

"No, this means that I can sit with you and Helen during the trial."

Sophie then called Tim, and said, "We might get the kids arraigned tomorrow."

"Have you contacted the Barton's yet?

"Yes, I have. I'm going to pick them up and we'll have breakfast before we go to the courthouse."

"Has anyone called the Marine Police Officer yet?"

"Nicole called him this morning and he's going to come over tonight and stay with a friend."

Tim said, "Sounds like everything is under control."

"I think it is and I'll call you and let you know how it went."

"Thanks Sophie, I'd appreciate that."

Just as she hung up with Tim, her phone rang, it was from Nicole, "Sophie, I received the warrants after lunch and the arraignment is scheduled for 9:00 tomorrow morning. Can you make sure that the Marine Police Officer gets the time?"

"I can do that. I called the Barton's yesterday and told them that I'd pick them up 7:00 and we'll have breakfast at Jimmy's."

"Can I join you for breakfast?"

"Of course, you can."

Sophie's last call for the day was to Matt Harris, "Matt, I'm calling to let you know the Judge scheduled the arraignment for Patrick and Simms for 9:00 tomorrow. I'm going to pick up Helen and Fred Barton to have breakfast at Jimmy's in Fells Point, please feel free to join us."

"Count me in."

She had a glass of wine and then went to bed.

<>

Sophie was up before the alarm sounded so she could pick up Helen and Fred on time. They were waiting for her, so they climbed into the car and she drove to Jimmy's in Fell's Point and she dropped them off at the door while she parked the car. Sophie walked with the Barton's into Jimmy's and found Nicole and Matt holding down a table for five. They did a round robin to introduce themselves.

No one would ever believe they were heading to a solemn and serious event as they chattered like Magpies sitting on an electric line.

Nicole announced, "It's time to go and the breakfast tab is on me. We'll meet in the lobby and walk to the courtroom together. This is the arraignment so we can sit together in the courtroom to hear the pleas and the probability of bail."

Sophie, Helen, and Fred Barton, along with Nicole and Matt entered and sat together on a bench midway to the Judge's Bench.

The group watched as Assistant US Attorney Stacy Greenwood entered the courtroom and walked to sit at the prosecutor's table.

Next to enter the courtroom was Federal Public Defender Patricia Adkins with George Patrick and Harold Simms. They sat at the defense table.

The bailiff entered the courtroom and called out, "Hear-ye – Hear-ye, all rise as the Honorable Adam Hammond enters the courtroom for case number 17-2541, arraignment of George Patrick and Harold Simms for violation of Title 21, US Code § 842 Drug Trafficking."

Judge Hammond asked for everyone to sit. He then asked the defendants to stand.

Federal Public Defender Patricia Adkins stood with the defendants.

Judge Hammond asked the defendants, "Please enter your plea for the charge of Drug Trafficking."

George Patrick waited quietly to hear what Harold said.

Harold Simms said, "Not Guilty."

George Patrick then followed Harold and said, "Not Guilty."

Judge Hammond said, "You may sit. He then asked Assistant US Attorney Greenwood, "Do you have a recommendation for bail?"

"Yes, Your Honor, the Government believes they are flight risks and recommend that they be returned to the Baltimore City Detention Center to await trial."

Hammond said, "The court marshals will return the defendants to the Baltimore City Detention Center, he then went on to say, Counselors, we will meet in this courtroom tomorrow morning at 9:00 am for the purpose of selecting a jury."

He then banged his gavel as he announced, "This court is now adjourned."

<>

In the morning, Fred Barton called Sophie and asked, "Helen and I can't attend anything in the courthouse today, can we?"

"No, we cannot, because the jury selection is taking place today."

"Sophie, I don't know how that works, can you please explain it to me?"

"Sure, at least 20 registered Maryland voters will enter the courtroom with a numbered placard given to them by the US Clerk's when they signed in. The sitting Judge, which in this case is Judge Adam Hammond, will take his seat on the bench to oversee the process. The Prosecutor, Stacy Greenwood, calls out a number first and asks one question then. Then the defense counsel, Patricia Adkins asks the same person a different question. The Defense starts the next round. They continue until they agree on fourteen jury Members. The Judge may call for a break to see how the attorneys are doing. They need to agree on all 14 numbers two of the numbers will sit as alternatives and not get a chance to vote unless a jury member needs to back out.

"Once they match, we have a jury, and at that point the judge releases the unchosen citizens and sends them to the Clerk's office to collect their checks."

"Sophie, are you saying that the folks who don't serve on the jury get paid?"

"Yes, because they weren't picked to serve on the jury, they registered with the Clerk's Office ready to do their civic duty by serving on a jury."

"Sophie thanks for explaining that."

"Not a problem, I'll call when I hear that we have a jury."

"That means the Helen and I can go to the grocery store."

"Yes, sir it does."

After disconnecting the call with Fred Barton, Sophie showered, dressed, and drove to her Office in Annapolis to meet with her boss and turn in her trip report.

Her boss, Joe Schofield said, "Sophie, I thought that I'd never see you again."

"Joe, there were times that I thought that I would never make it back home. The worst part of the investigation is that we never nailed down the person who ran the drug ring demanding the two bandits who are just kids who both said they were the walking dead because they didn't get the drugs delivered on time. We did get the conviction for First Degree Murder in Crisfield. Joe they are babies who will now spend the rest of the life in prison on the murder charges and to make it worse in my mind whoever their boss is will have them killed in prison."

Sophie, "I'm sure that you're on the right track about that, but you got the right information to the right people and no one can ask for more than that."

"Joe, I hear what you're saying, but there's a bastard out there preying on young children to do his dirty work by putting the fear of being murdered by his hand in them."

Joe asked, "Is it safe to assume that you'll be attending the drug trial?"

"That's right and I'll be taking the victim's parents in my murder case to the drug trafficking trial."

"Just don't get yourself killed because you're irreplaceable."

"I'm going to take as a compliment."

"You should because it was."

Sophie left her office and went to the grocery store because as the say goes, just like Old Mother Hubbard her cupboards were as bare as the children's story, so were Sophie's.

She'd just put the last item when her phone rang. It was Nicole who said, "We have a jury and the trial will begin tomorrow at 9:00."

Sophie asked, "Have you called Matt yet?"

"Not yet, but let me ask, do we want the whole group to meet as Jimmies first?"

"Yes, and I'll make the calls. She called the Barton's and Matt Harris to let them know that the trial starts tomorrow and for everyone to meet at Jimmies for breakfast."

Chapter Six

While eating breakfast, everyone looked a bit nervous, but no one said a word. Nicole and Sophie had excellent intuition, so they glanced at one another knowing they were on the same page.

Nicole paid the breakfast tab and as they walk the door, said, "My gut is telling me that we're walking into a raging storm."

Sophie said, "Mine is as well."

They drove to the courthouse and once everyone cleared the security checkpoint, Nicole led them to the elevator and punched the 7th floor button. The courtroom doors were locked, so they waited in the hall and that made the Barton's nervous.

Fred asked Sophie, "Are the courtroom doors for the federal court routinely locked?"

"Yes, they are, and the reason is to keep the courtroom safe. The bailiff will shortly unlock the doors and then we can go in and sit."

Fred then asked, "Where are Patrick and Simms?"

"Deputy US Marshals will pick them up from the Baltimore City Detention Center and bring them to the courthouse's lockup. Traffic can delay the effort."

The courtroom door opened, and the bailiff asked, "I need to ask Assistant US Attorney Stacey Greenwood and Federal Public Defender Patricia Adkins to follow me to the Judge Adam Hammond's Office."

There wasn't much conversation in the hallway. Helen Barton was so nervous that her husband held her close to him for fear that she'd fall.

Nicole eased her way over to Sophie and said quietly, "I've never seen this happen before."

Sophie quietly responded, "Neither have I. Fred Barton is holding Helen up, so I hope this waiting doesn't go on for much longer."

Inside Judge Hammond's Chambers, he was explaining to the attorneys, "The transport car was ambushed both defendants, Patrick and Simms sustained major injuries. Deputy US August Bennet sustained near fatal injuries. Deputy US Marshal Alec Tailor managed to shoot both persons in the attacking car. Everyone was taken to the University of Maryland Shock Trauma Center. I believe that it's prudent to wait and see how injured Patrick and Simms are before we continue this trial."

Assistant US Attorney Greenwood asked, "Your Honor, can we move forward to investigate who ordered the hit?"

"Those are a prudent request, but let's wait to hear what the US Deputy Marshals say first."

"Thank you, Your Honor."

Greenwood and Adkins exited the courtroom together and asked everyone to follow them to the conference room.

Assistant US Attorney Stacy Greenwood said, "Please help yourself to the coffee and donuts while I explain what I know so far."

Nicole and Sophie sat together thinking that their guts had told them that this was going to be a bad day.

Greenwood opened the conversation by saying, "The transport car to bring Patrick and Simms to the courthouse was ambushed by unknown persons in another car. Deputy US Marshal Alec Taylor managed to shoot and kill the two perpetrators. Deputy US Marshal Albert Baylor and the two defendants, Patrick and Simms were injured and are currently in the Maryland Medical Center's Shock Trauma unit."

Nicole asked, "Is it possible that this was a hit job?"

"Anything is possible, but until we know more, we need to sit tight and wait. I know that you don't wait well, but I also know that you want a successful completion to this case."

Nicole then asked, "Will you go to the hospital?"

"It's likely that I will as soon as the doctor says I can."

Nicole pushed the issue by saying, "The longer we wait to start find the person or persons means they'll have the ability to run or worse yet, order hits on more folks associated with his business."

"Nicole, I agree with you, but the judge told me to wait."

"Isn't Judge Hammond aware of the consequences of waiting?"

"Nicole, my position would be at risk if I challenged the judge."

"I know, so, I'll let it rest."

"I'll call as soon as I know more."

<>

Everyone left the conference room bewildered by what they'd heard.

To break the silence, Fred said, "I believe it's my turn to pick up the tab for lunch, so where does everyone want to go?"

Sophie said, "Since the cars are parked in a garage that's paid for the day, why don't we walk to the Pratt Street Ale House?"

The tables were set up for four diners, so Matt borrowed an empty chair.

The ladies ordered wine while the gents ordered draft beer. They ordered lunch from the menu."

Fred asked Nicole, "Do you have any idea how long the wait will be?"

"Fred, I don't, because I've never seen this happen before, which means that I'm in the dark just like everyone else. We'll get a call and then we'll know what's going on."

"Any suggestions for what Helen and I do in the meantime?"

"Fred, the only suggestion I can make is to back to your routine, and I'll make sure that you get an update if I hear anything."

At that moment, Nicole's cell phone rang, it was Stacy, "Nicole, I need you to come to my office."

Nicole said to the folks standing around, "That was Stacey Greenwood, asking me to come to her office."

Sophie asked, "Did she say what it was about?"

"No, she didn't"

Matt said, "I'll stick around for a while and if nothing comes of it, I'm gonna go home."

Sophie, Fred, and Helen agreed with him.

<>

Inside the Court's Conference Room were Stacey Greenwood and Deputy US Marshal Alec Taylor. Greenwood made the introductions and turned the conversation over to Taylor.

Taylor explained, "I shot both men in the assaulting car and had the Coroner's van pick them up to take then to Medical Examiner located in the mortuary. I then ran the plate to learn that the car was a rental out of New Jersey, rented with cash under the name of Antonio Rizzo. At this point, I'm turning over this over to the FBI. Agent Andrea York has been assigned to the case."

Greenwood said, "Thank you Marshal Taylor, you have been most helpful, and I'll contact Agent York."

Nicole added. "I'll help as much as I can."

<>

Nicole waited until she was home to call both Sophie and Matt to update them.

Matt said, "I'm gonna go back to work, but call me if you need me."

Sophie called the Barton's to give them the update.

Fred asked, "Do you have any idea how long this might take?"

"No. I don't because a new case might be evolving at this point.

Chapter Seven

Assistant US Attorney Stacy Greenwood called FBI Agent Andrea York and asked, "Agent York is it possible for you to meet with Drug Enforcement Agent Nicole Hensley, who's been involved in the trafficking case from the beginning?"

York said, "I can do that since Agent Hensley works for the Drug Enforcement Agency, she knows more about this case than I do which means I can learn a lot from her."

"Andrea, she's really a good teacher."

Andrea took Greenwood's advice and called DEA Agent Nicole Hensley, who answered on the first ring. "This is Nicole Hensley; how may I help you?"

"My name is Andrea York and Assistant US Attorney Stacy Greenwood suggested that I call you to help with your case. Can we meet for lunch?"

"Yes, and I would include FBI Agent Sophie Brock in the Marine Crime Forensic Lab because she opened this case and knows more than I do."

"Agent Hensley, can you call her and invite her to lunch with us?"

Nicole called Sophie, "We have a new member of the team, her name is Andrea York and we're planning to have lunch together and would like you to join us."

"Nicole while I'm excited about the additional help, who is she and what will she bring to this case?"

"I really don't know, but AUSA Stacy Greenwood called her and suggested that she call me."

They decided to meet at the Federal House Bar and Grill, and during lunch, York said, "I'm sitting with two lunch mates who are well versed in this case and I'm nervous because Greenwood did not brief me on it."

Nicole said, "I'm not sure how much she actually knows, so we'll tell you what we know, and the best approach is to start at the beginning. Sophie, I think since you started the investigation on the two defendants. George Patrick and Harold Simms, you should go first."

"I was called in to investigate two dead bodies found in their boat. Fingerprints matched with the report I ran through NCIS for George Patrick and Harold Simms. Simms is definitely the brighter of the two, but both agreed that they were the walking dead because they didn't deliver the package on time. Marine Officer Matt Harris caught them transferring cocaine from one boat to another and took them into custody. The first-degree murder trial was heard in Crisfield, Maryland and a jury came in with a guilty verdict. The Judge sentenced them to life without the benefit of parole."

Nicole picked up where Sophie left off. "The Judge in Crisfield had two Deputy US Marshals ready to transport the two defendants to the Baltimore City Detention Center and I heard what Sophie heard about the fact that the two defendants would be murdered before the trial. Both are in the hospital in critical condition, which means I really believe that they won't make it to trial."

York added, "That means we're starting from scratch."

Sophie said, "If we can't get at least one of the defendants to give us something to work with, we're gonna be in a pickle."

York said, "We need to follow the money because that's a key component in solving this case."

They walked to the Federal House Bar and Grill for lunch and during lunch the conversation surrounded the fact that they weren't following the money.

They ordered a round of coffee along with a dessert to develop a plan. Nicole would requisition two cars from the Drug Enforcement Evidence Lab and Sophie would follow the car carrying the suspected drugs and cash and report the destination to Nicole, so she and Andrea could take over the surveillance.

They were pleased with their plan, so Andrea paid the tab and walked to the parking garage across from the courthouse and said, "I think this will work well."

Sophie called Joe Schofield, "Joe, we now have three agents working on this case, and we plan to follow the money, to see where it leads before making any arrests."

"Sophie, how is related to your job?"

"I took them to court in Crisfield and they were both convicted of First-Degree Murder. They were both wanted for drug trafficking, so they were transported to Baltimore, to stand trial. While being transported from the Baltimore City Detention to the US District Court on Lombard Street, someone attacked the car. One of the Marshals and the two defendants are currently in the hospital."

"Sophie, I'm not sure that I want you in the middle of this, but you seem set to do it. Please keep me up to date."

"I will, Joe."

<>

Nicole called her supervisor Richard Young, to update him on the plan that was created over lunch.

"Nicole, while that sounds like a good plan to you, it makes me nervous to think that three women are planning to execute an unsafe plan, which means if you get caught, the three of you could end up dead."

"Richard, would you feel less nervous, if I called my old partner Garret Sherman?"

"It might, but don't con him into working on your case, because I keep him busy."

"Richard, this will turn into a very large case, if everything goes as planned."

"I'm sure it will, so make sure you check in with me regularly."

She then called her old partner, DEA Agent Garrett Sherwood, "Garrett, we have a situation and we have a plan. I would appreciate your thoughts on it."

Nicole started with the murder case and ended with the transport car being assaulted and the fact that there were now three folks in the hospital.

"Our plan is to follow the money and arrest the bandits supplying the drugs."

"Nicole, I've always considered you as a smart and intelligent woman; however, that plan will place all of you in dangerous territory. I have a recommendation for you, that you can take or not, have two agents follow you.

<>

Nicole, Sophie, and Andrea met for breakfast and made the decision to canvas one area to watch for drug traffic.

Nicole added her piece by saying, "I talked with my ex-partner yesterday. He offered to a backup team follow a good distance behind us, to help if we get into a problem.

Sophie and Andrea agreed that it was a great idea.

Nicole contacted Garret, "The team loves your idea."

Garret then said, "Before you leave, please make sure you put a tracking device on the car."

"I will and I'll also make sure it's working, so watch for it."

She'd requisitioned a car from the DEA's confiscated vehicle pool. While she activated the tracking device, she explained what she was doing. "All confiscated vehicles are equipped with a tracking device and I'm activating the device now, so Garret knows where we are at all times."

She drove past the site several times, hoping to look like three lost women. When she finally pulled to the side of the street, she hoped liked hell that as white woman she looked forlorn as she stopped to ask for directions to a place she knew well.

The guy came over to the car and thought she looked as though she wanted to score, but when she only asked for directions, he gave them to her.

Nicole thanked him and drove away and parked the car on a coffee shop lot. They went in to grab a cup of coffee and assess this morning's outing.

Sophie said, "I think it went well, because as you were driving around watching for the opportunity to ask for directions. I watched a number of deals take place."

Andrea asked, "What's the next step?'

"Tomorrow I'll requisition two cars and tag team the two cars to see where the money's going and it's likely that a buy will take place."

Andrea asked, "Why can't we them for a big buy, like a couple kilos?

Nicole said, "Seriously do the three of us look like we'd buy cocaine by the kilo?"

Sophie asked Andrea, "How many drug deals have you been involved with"

"I have to say, none this close to the crime."

"What is your position with the FBI?"

"I'm an accountant, so I traced the money the agents bring in for all sorts of crimes."

Sophie and Nicole looked one another, and Nicole said, "Andrea then that's your task on this case, our goal is find the money trail to the top person who's calling the shots."

"I'm so happy to have a real job on this case. Listening to the two of you talk, I was sure that I would be useless."

Sophie said, "We thought that as well, but welcome to the team."

Nicole said, "I do as well."

Nicole had requisitioned two cars from the DEA confiscated vehicle pool and initiated the tracking devices.

Before pulling out of the lot, Nicole called Garret to let him know that they were getting on the road.

Nicole said, "Andrea, you'll ride with me.

Chapter Eight

Garret called Nicole to say, "I can see both cars and the tracking devices are working. I've commandeered a co-pilot, whose name is Frank Walden, he's a DEA Agent."

Nicole responded with, "That's great. Sophie is ahead of us waiting on a parking lot."

"I've got her on the tracking device window in my car."

Andrea said, "Nicole, one of the dealers just got into a light blue Honda Accord with North Carolina, First in -Flight Plates, Number B79*48."

Nicole said, "Andrea take my phone and call both Sophie and Garret to let them know, just remember the phone is set up for a conference call."

"This is Andrea York, and I just observed two of the drug dealers get into a light blue Honda Accord with North Carolina First In-Flight Plates – Number B79*48."

Nicole watched as Sophie fell in behind her car and at that moment, she didn't see Garrett, but knew he was behind her. She followed the bandit's car to Wilmington and told Sophie to take the lead.

Nicole moved into the right lane and watched as Sophie's car passed her.

Sophie followed the car into a service area in New Jersey. She looked into review mirror and put lipstick on, she said, "The Blue Honda is parked two spaces away from me."

Garrett said, "Sophie, sit tight, we're almost there."

So that she didn't look obvious, she grabbed a map from the glove box and pretended to read it. Out of the corner of her eye, she watched a black Pontiac Grand park next to the car she'd been following. The windows were down on both cars, so she watched as they exchanged what looked to her like money for cocaine.

Holding the map up, she said, "Garrett, I think the deal is going down in this service area."

Nicole said, "I'm turning onto the lot."

Garrett said, "Sophie see if you can keep an eye on them until Frank and I get there, were about five minutes out."

Sophie said, "Garrett, in five minutes, the deal will be done, and they'll be gone."

"Sophie, we see the cars now and we'll take them into custody. We're pulling onto the lot as we speak. Nicole, see if you can block them until Frank and I get there."

Nicole pulled the car behind the two suspected cars and Andrea went inside the service area and grabbed two cups of coffee and while she was getting the coffees the suspects were fenced in.

By the time Garrett and Frank arrived there was a great deal of horn honking along with shouts of profanity at the women blocking them in.

Garrett chuckled as he added his car to the line.

He asked the two men in the car closest to him, to step out of the car.

Frank asked the men closest to him to step out of the car.

Garrett then said, "Ladies, the cars are yours for a look to see what we have so far."

Sophie came up with the cocaine while Nicole found the bag of money.

Garrett said, "I'll order the tow trucks and have the cars towed to the DEA Lab in Baltimore. Nicole please call Stacey Greenwood to see where she wants the four new bandits."

Greenwood asked, "Have they been mirandized?"

"No, they have not."

"In that case take them to the Baltimore City Detention Center and call me when they arrive."

"Greenwood said to deliver the bandits to the Baltimore City Detention Center, and I'll call her when they arrive."

Garrett said, "The tow trucks should arrive in about 20 minutes, so he and Frank would wait for them to take to DEA's forensic lab."

The tow trucks arrived and towed the cars to DEA's crime lab, so Garrett and Frank drove to the Baltimore City Detention Center to drop off the two bandits. After they were turned over to the officials, Garrett called Nicole, "Your bandits were delivered to the Baltimore Detention Center."

"Thanks Garrett, I'll call AUSA Greenwood and let her know they were delivered."

Greenwood asked, "Does anyone know their names?"

"I don't and I doubt that Garrett or Frank does.

"The car windows were down, so we were able to watch the money passed from one car to the other for the suspected cocaine. After Garrett and Frank took them into custody, Sophie found the cocaine in one of the cars and I found money in the other car."

Stacey said, "Let's get them at least Mirandized and once we know what we have in terms of the amount of cocaine and money, I'll get a warrant."

"Andrea is working on the amount of both cash and cocaine that we brought from the scene. Stacey thanks you for referring her to us for this case."

"Nicole, she good at what she does, so as soon as we a name for each bandit, along with fingerprints, she'll let us know what's going on."

Garrett called Nicole, "The cars are ready to be thoroughly investigated."

"I'll give Sophie a call and send her over."

Sophie said, "Not a problem. Let Garrett know that I'm on my way."

Garrett was waiting for her at the vehicle lab and asked, "Sophie is there anything you need."

"I don't think so. Are you planning to stick around?

"Yes, I'll stay with you until you're done."

Sophie said, "Thank you I appreciate it." She then grabbed and started with fingerprints. She dusted the Honda Accord and put the fingerprints on a piece of tape and then put them in a bag she labeled 'Honda'. Next was the Pontiac and a labeled the bag.

Once that was done, she asked Garrett. "Can you run these for a match and for their names?"

He took the prints from her and digitized them for the computer. They matched

- George Beardsley, 42 years old. Spent time in prison for drug trafficking.
- Christopher Wade, 32 years old. He had a juvenile record for murdering the neighbor's dog.
- Ronald Tyson, 50 years old. Wanted for a parole violation in Boston, Massachusetts for the murder of his wife.
- Ted Swift, 22 years old, has a clean record

Sophie found traces of cocaine in both cars and put them in a baggy for each car, she took what she had and went looking for Garrett to give him the baggies.

<>

While waiting for the results from the two vehicles, Nicole asked Greenwood, "Where are Patrick and Simms?"

"When they were released from the hospital, they were re-located to a safe house while we looked for the suspects."

Nicole then asked about the injured Deputy US Marshal.

"When he was released from the hospital, he was retired from the service will full retirement benefits that included health care."

<>

Sophie called Nicole, "I'm going to e-mail you what Garrett uncovered from their fingerprints and I'll bring the bagged evidence wherever you want them."

"Thanks Sophie, ask Garret if he can put them in the evidence locker while I check to what Greenwood wants to do."

Nicole called Stacey, "The bandits are in the Baltimore City Detention Center. Sophie sent me the fingerprints via e-mail, so I'll forward them to you."

Stacey told her, "Why don't you meet me there with the evidence you have and after they've been Mirandized, I'll get warrants for drug trafficking."

They arrived at the Detention Center at the same time. Stacy signed in on the log and Nicole followed her.

The four bandits were delivered to the interview by two Detention Guards. They were seated across from one another on the sides of the table with Stacey Greenwood and Nicole Hensley on the ends.

Stacey Greenwood mirandized them one at a time starting with George Beardsley, who according to the RAP sheet forwarded to her spent time in prison for drug trafficking. After reading him his Miranda rights, she asked him to sign the Miranda form.

Next was Christopher Wade who according to the RAP sheet has a juvenile record for killing the neighbor's dog. She read him his rights and asked him to sign the Miranda form.

Her third bandit was Ronald Tyson who was wanted for a parole violation in Boston, Massachusetts for the murder of his wife. She gave him a hard look as she read him his rights and signed the Miranda form.

The last bandit she read the Miranda Rights to was Ted Swift and he had a clean record as he signed the form, Stacey wondered how he got involved in drug trafficking, but he did.

After Mirandizing them, Stacey asked, "Do you have an attorney?"

In unison, they said, "Antonio De Luca."

That name was music to her ears because he was the mob's lawyer. She left the room and asked the guard to provide the four defendants a phone to call their attorney.

Stacey then called Judge Morgan Bedford and requested four warrants for drug trafficking

His secretary said, "Ms. Greenwood. The warrants will be ready to pick up in a half-hour."

Stacy asked Nicole, "Can you please pick the warrants up from Judge Bedford's chambers in about a half-hour?"

"I'll go up now and wait for them."

De Luca arrived and asked Greenwood, "What have my clients been charged with?"

She told him, "Drug trafficking and the arrest warrants are on their way, signed by Judge Bedford."

De Luca went into the interview room and closed the door behind him. He angrily asked "Can someone explain what happened and why you were taken into custody for drug trafficking?

The four defendants stared at the table-top and not one said a word.

De Luca said with that same angry voice, "I'm not a happy man at the moment and I have to assume that you were sloppy, which means that I'm tempted to walk out the door and leave you to fend for yourselves because there was a large amount of money involved in that transaction. Money, you will pay back with your life."

Beardsley said, "The transfer was going fine until a car boxed us in."

De Luca said, "If you are convicted of drug trafficking, it'll be the third time and that means you will spend the rest of your life in prison and I'm gonna say, it will be a short life for you.

He went on to say, "A lot of money and drugs were confiscated which means you lost it and can't get it back. I'll defend you because that's what I'm paid to do, but if you screw up in the courtroom, we'll all end up as fish food, do you understand what I'm saying?"

They nodded their heads.

Greenwood tapped on the interview room door and then went in to tell De Luca, "I have the warrants for arrest signed by The Honorable Gerald Chaney. He asked how many days you need to review the evidence before he set the arraignment date."

"How soon can I have it, along with the list of prosecutor's witnesses?"

"I'll have everything sent to you by messenger this afternoon by 5:00 pm."

De Luca said, "I'll need a day to review everything."

The Prosecuting team had lunch and then went home.

De Luca met with the defendants in the Detention Center where he told them, "Things are not looking good for the four of you."

They hung their heads low knowing that they had no chance in hell of staying alive until their next birthday. If De Luca was able to get an acquittal for them, there would be hit men waiting to take them out. If on the other hand, they were found guilty, there would be other inmates to take care of the situation and the prison guards would just watch as they were killed.

De Luca left the detention center and had a drink in a downtown bar before he drove home.

<>

In the morning, everyone and anyone related to this case arrived at the US District Court in Baltimore, Maryland. After passing through the security checkpoint located just inside the front door, everyone, including De Luca made their way up the elevator to the seventh floor where the courtroom was located.

When the courtroom doors were unlocked, Greenwood went in to sit at the Prosecutor's table and the De Luca sat at the Defense table to wait for his clients to be brought in from the courthouse lockup.

Andrea York, Nicole Hensley, Sophie Brock, Garret Sherwood, and Frank Walden were witnesses which meant they had to wait in the hallway until called into the courtroom.

De Luca stood as his clients were brought into the courtroom and sat to his left.

The Bailiff entered the crowded courtroom and called out "Hear-ye Hear ye, will everyone
stand as The Honorable Gerald Chaney enters the courtroom for the arraignment of the Government vs. George Beardsley, Christopher Wade, Ronald Tyson and Ted Swift, case number 17-7472 for drug trafficking, in violation if of Title 21 US Code § 841."

Judge Chaney sat and asked for everyone to be seated.

He then asked, "Will the defendants please stand."

De Luca stood as well.

De Luca was shocked to see that a jury had been assigned without his knowledge. He stood to address the Judge, "Your Honor, I was not aware that this would be a jury trial."

The Judge said, "Mr. De Luca, if you prefer, I will dismiss the jury and I will hear the case."

While De Luca wanted to oppose the jury, he knew he had a better chance with a jury. He was pissed that he wasn't aware a jury had been selected but knew he could use that information to get his defendants off by claiming a mistrial, because he wasn't aware that a jury had been appointed.

De Luca said, "Your Honor, while I was unaware that a jury had been assigned, I will not ask that the charges be dismissed, and my clients will be heard before a jury of their peers."

Now that his statement was part of the record, he repeated, "Your Honor, I appreciate that my defendants will be heard by a jury of their peers."

"Thank you, counselor, will you have a problem if I ask your clients how they plead?"

De Luca knew the judge was being cantankerous because he knew who De Luca represented.

"No, Your Honor, I don't have a problem with it."

Chaney went down the line and asked each of the four defendants how they pled, all four responded, "Not Guilty."

The Judge then asked Greenwood, "Does the Government have a recommendation for bail?"

"Yes, Your Honor, it does. The defendants are a flight risk as well as drug traffickers, so the Government recommends that they be held without the benefit of posting bail."

"So noted, the defendants will remain in custody without the benefit of posting bail. Is the Government prepared to show probable cause?"

"Yes, Your Honor it is."

"Then please proceed."

Greenwood walked to the middle of the courtroom and faced the jury. "The Government has evidence and testimony to show that the defendants paid $200,000 for 1 kilo of cocaine. The street value on cut and packaged cocaine amounts to over one million dollars. We have witnesses who will testify as to their role in the investigation."

The Judge said, "Thank you, Ms. Greenwood. The court is going to take a 15-minute break and after, the Government will call its first witness to the stand."

The bailiff called out, "This Court is now in session."

Judge Chaney announced from his bench, "The Government will call its first witness to the stand."

The Government calls for Andrea York of the Federal Bureau to the stand. The bailiff went out to the hall and said, "Ms. York, you're up." She followed him into the courtroom and ended at the witness chair. The bailiff asked York to put her hand on the bible he held and then said, "Do you promise to tell the whole truth, so help you God."

Greenwood asked if she could state her full name for the record.

"My full name is Andrea Lynn York."

"Ms. York, are you employed?"

"Yes, I work for the FBI and I assess the money and/or drugs confiscated in each case and log the amounts and place them in the evidence room."

"Ms. York, were you involved in this case?"

"Yes, I was. I wrote a report that contained the $200,000.00 cash and one kilo of cocaine."

Greenwood pulled the report from her briefcase and walked it to the witness stand. "Is this the report you wrote?"

"Yes, it is."

Greenwood then took the report to De Luca to show him.

Greenwood then said, "Your Honor, I have no more questions for this witness."

Judge Chaney asked, "Mr. De Luca would you like to cross-examine this witness?"

"Yes, Your Honor, I would."

He stood from the defense table and walked to the witness stand. Andrea saw how evil his eyes were before he asked her, "Can you prove the items in you report, are in fact actual evidence?"

"Yes, Drug Enforcement Agent Garrett handed me the bag of money he'd taken from defendant George Beardsley and Drug Enforcement Agent Frank Walden handed me the kilo of cocaine; he'd taken from defendant Christopher Wade."

"Ms. York are you certain without a shred of doubt that is what happened?"

"Yes, Mr. De Luca, I am because I was there and watched with my eyes."

"Your Honor, I have no more questions for this witness."

Judge Chaney looked at her with kind eyes as he said, "Ms. York, you may step down and since you testified, you may remain in the courtroom, for the rest of the trial."

York stepped down from the witness chair and walked to the last bench in the room.

The Judge asked, "Will the Government please call its next witness to the stand?"

Greenwood called for Garret Sherwood to come to the witness stand.

The bailiff went into the hall to call for Sherwood, "You're up."

After the bailiff swore him in, Greenwood asked him, "Can you state your full name for the record?"

"My name is Garrett James Sherwood."

"Mr. Sherwood are you currently employed?"

"Yes, I work as an agent with the Drug Enforcement Agency."

"Agent Sherwood, were you involved in this case?"

"Yes, I was."

"Please explain the nature of your involvement."

"I trained Agent Nicole Hensley in the Drug Enforcement Agency and then we became partners. She called me to ask my opinion about her plan, which was working with an FBI agent and an FBI marine forensic specialist; the plan was to follow a car that they suspected to have money and have a second car further back, so they could tag team the suspected money car. I told her that sending three women out to chase drug runners was a bad plan. A better one would be for me to follow them along with DEA Agent Frank Walden. Using mobile phones set up for conferencing, Sophie Brock, notified everyone that the car she'd been following pulled off in a New Jersey Service Area. She told me that the occupants of the first car went into the store, so I told her to follow them in, giving the rest of our cars time to get in position. Frank and I along with Nicole and

Andrea watched a black Pontiac Grand Am pull in next to the Light Blue Honda Accord with North Carolina First license plates. The two government cars blocked them and watched as bags were exchanged from one car to the next. Walden took the Pontiac and asked the two folks to step out and recovered a bag of cash from the passenger, while I recovered a kilo of cocaine from the Honda's passenger. We gave Andrea York the recovered bags and then waited for tow trucks to arrive to tow the cars to the Drug Enforcement Forensic Lab."

Judge Chaney asked, "Mr. De Luca would you like to cross-examine this witness?"

De Luca stood and said "Yes, Your Honor, I would. He walked the witness stand where he asked, "Agent Sherwood, are you aware that you do not have the authority to search a personal vehicle without a warrant?"

"Mr. De Luca, we did not search the vehicles until the stolen cars were in the DEA's vehicle forensic lab with a warrant signed by Judge Chaney."

"Agent Sherwood, did you at any time tell my clients that they were under arrest?"

"No, we were instructed to deliver the defendants to the Baltimore City Detention Center."

"Your Honor, I have no more questions for this witness."

Judge Chaney asked, "Does the Government have any witnesses to call to the stand?"

"No, Your Honor, it does not. Does the Defense have any witnesses to call to the stand?"

"No, Your Honor, it does not."

Chaney addressed the courtroom, "We will take a one-hour recess for lunch. The bailiff will lead the jury into the jury room for lunch. I'm going to caution the jurors not to discuss this case during lunch.

The prosecuting team walked to Frank and Nicks West end Grille.

When it was time to go, they walked back to hear the closing summaries. The courtroom was crowded with the press and courthouse employees.

Sophie Brock, Nicole Hensley, Garrett Sherwood, and Frank Walden stood along the back wall since there wasn't anywhere to sit. The watched as sketch artists pulled drawing pads out to be ready for the Closing Summaries.

Antonio De Luca was up first, he stood and then walked to the jury box where he said, "The jury members look to be fine and knowledgeable folks who, like me, found a number of holes and outright lies from the Prosecutor's case and put reasonable doubt in my mind by saying that my clients were drug trafficking criminals. Please look at them at table all dressed in suits, looking like businessmen who were conducting business in a New Jersey Service Center and were wrongfully taken into custody by the Federal Government. If you agree with me, you must vote for an acquittal."

He then walked back to the defense table and sat.

Stacey Greenwood stood and walked to stand in front of the defendants. "The four defendants are dressed in business suits, because they are businessmen. They are in the business of drug trafficking and very much want to look like businessmen and not junkies: however, you heard testimony and evidence to support that testimony. You must return a guilty verdict, so children don't die anymore because of illegal drugs."

Greenwood then returned to sit at the prosecutor's table

Judge Chaney asks the Jury, "Do the Jury member wish to continue and deliberate today?"

They nodded their heads indicating the wanted to move on to the deliberation process.

The Bailiff led them to the jury room, where non-alcoholic beverages were in a bowl of ice along with an assortment of sliced fruit.

Judge Chaney entered the room to instruct the jury, "First is to appoint a foreman to represent you and direct questions through the bailiff to me. You will select 12 members to serve as jurors and 2 to serve as alternates in the event a juror cannot continue. It's important to take your time and debate the issues of this case before voting. Make certain that you understand fully the charges. All questions are sent by the foreman to the bailiff who will bring them to me."

Judge Chaney left the jury room to wait in his chambers.

The media chose to wait in the courtroom. The prosecution witnesses walked to the Kona Grill and over coffee they congratulated one another over how well they did on the stand, no matter how hard De Luca pushed them.

Greenwood called Nicole to let everyone know that the jury's in.

Chapter Nine

The courtroom was more crowded than when they left for lunch. In order to get inside the courtroom, the taller folks stood against the back wall with the shorter folks in front of them, so that everyone could what was happening.

Judge Chaney asked, "Has the jury reached a verdict?"

The foreman said, "Yes, Your Honor, it has."

"Please hand it to the bailiff."

The bailiff handed it to the Judge who looked at it and then handed it back to the bailiff and he handed it to the Foreman.

The Foreman read aloud, "One the charge of Drug Trafficking, we find defendant George Beardsley guilty. On the charge of Drug Trafficking, we find Christopher Wade guilty, on the charge of Drug Trafficking, we find Ronald Tyson guilty. On the charge of Drug Trafficking, we find Ted Swift guilty."

He then sat.

The Judge said, "I would like to thank the jury for performing its civic duty by answering your notice to become a part of the jury. I am releasing you from the jury; your checks are available in the Clerk's office."

Chaney waited until all of the jurors left the courtroom, to ask, "Mr. Beardsley, please stand."

De Luca stood with his client.

The Judge said, "This is your third offense for dealing in drugs, which means that I have no choice in the sentence. You are hereby sentenced to life, without the benefit of parole. You may sit."

Judge Chaney asked, "Mr. Wade, please stand."

De Luca stood with his client.

The Judge said, "Mr. Wade you should have chosen an honest job rather than drug trafficking and harming animals. I'm sentencing you to life. You may sit."

"Mr. Tyson, there are two Deputy US Marshals here in the courthouse waiting to take you back to Boston, Massachusetts, for parole violation."

"Mr. Swift, please stand."

De Luca stood with his client.

"Mr. Swift, you are much too young to spend the rest of your life in prison, but that's what's gonna happen, because I'm sentencing to 50 years."

Judge Chaney announced, "I have asked the Department of Corrections to house you in separate prisons."

The media trampled down folks to get the story out first, not appearing to care who they hurt in the stampede.

Nicole, Sophie, Andrea, Garret and Frank remained plastered to the back wall until the courtroom cleared. They stepped into the deserted hall to hear what they believed were either cars or trucks back-firing. Nicole pushed the down button on the elevator, but it never came.

Garrett said, "Maybe we heard a transformer blow, so let's take the stairs." The stairs were locked.

The courthouse had a wall of glass, so they made their way to the window, but the only thing they would see were fire trucks, rescue vehicles and police cars.

Judge Chaney made his way to them and said, "Defense attorney De Luca was shot and died on the spot, in the middle of Lombard Street, presumably on his way to the garage. I have no idea how long the courthouse is going to be in a lockdown, but if you want, you are welcome to join me in my office where I a coffee pot which means I can make a fresh pot of coffee."

He poured everyone a cup of coffee.

As she was sipping her hot coffee, Sophie asked, "Your Honor, did the defendants get out of the building?"

"Yes, they did Ms. Brock."

With a quiet voice Nicole said, "De Luca said if he didn't get acquittals, he would be taken down."

"Ms. Hensley, the jury came in with a guilty verdict on a four defendants. I had nothing to do with it."

Her voice remained quiet as she said, "I understand Your Honor."

Everyone heard a fire marshal as he said. "All is clear, and the elevators are operational."

They stood and thanked Judge Chaney for his hospitality and then left the courthouse to go home.

<>

Greenwood called every member of her team and them and her team she made dinner reservations at McCormick and Schmitt's for 7:00 that evening.

After showering and dressing for dinner, they made their way to the restaurant.

The hostess showed them to the table where US Attorney Theodore Chennault and Assistant US Attorney Stacey Greenwood were seated. They sat at the table and ordered drinks.

When the drinks arrived, US Attorney Chennault said, "I asked Stacey if I could join everyone for dinner to congratulate everyone on a job well done."

Everyone thanked him for his complimenting their work.

Nicole asked, "What happens now that De Luca was shot in the middle of the street and died there?"

Chennault said, "We'll open a new case; however, this investigation doesn't die, because De Luca was murdered. You gave us a crack in the door to investigate up a level."

Sophie asked, "Will this team be a part of the new investigation?"

"I hope that everyone will stay on."

"Mr. Chennault, do you know what will happen to Patrick and Simms?"

"They have been placed in the Witness Protection Program.

Now that they knew the kids were safe, the conversation transformed from work to telling jokes and lots of good-hearted laughter.

Stacey paid the bill and after thanking her for a great dinner, her team made their way home and waited for the late news to come on. Regardless of the network channel you chose, De Luca was the leading story. The commentators said that he was shot down in the middle of Lombard Street in Baltimore, Maryland.

They went on in their opinion to keep the public safe, to say that Antonio De Luca was in their opinion, a crime boss's attorney and at the point, if you changed the channel; the commentators speculated the reason for the drive-by murder, creating a number of different speculations.

<>

In the morning, Stacey called her team members to meet in her office at 10:00.

Once they were crammed onto her small office. She asked them, "Follow me to the conference room, where there's more room at the table and fresh coffee along with cinnamon buns."

Before sitting, everyone grabbed a fresh cup of coffee along with a cinnamon bun.

Stacey opened the meeting, with, "US Attorney Theodore Chennault has charged us with taking this case to the next level. Andrea, with your financial skills, would you look into the money laundering for this case?"

"Yes, I can do that."

"Thank you, it'll be a huge help."

"Next, since you did such a great job of finding the buys and following the car to the pickup and drop-off location might be us new folks to watch."

"Last, I believe that weekly meetings away from the courthouse and my office might be in order. If anyone feels the need to meet face-to-face, pick a location and we'll meet there."

Nicole asked, "When do we start?"

Stacey told her, "Tomorrow. Find a place to have breakfast, so you can talk over the day."

<>

In the morning, after a number phone calls back and forth to one another the team agreed to meet at Jimmy's in Fells Point for breakfast. Nicole searched for a table that five folks could sit at; it meant pushing two tables for four. That worked perfectly when Garrett brought in a guy they hadn't met before.

Garrett made the instructions to the team, "Please raise your hand as I introduce you. First is Nicole Hensley, next is Sophie Brock, and then Andrea York. You know Frank. This is Don Yarrow, who works in the DEA Accounting Department."

Andrea's eyes lit up as she asked, "Garrett, will Don Yarrow be working with me?"

"Don's gonna make a great co-pilot for you, so you won't be working alone."

Don and Andrea nodded to one another.

Nicole suggested, "Why don't we use the conference call setting that they used yesterday and start in the same location to see if business has resumed normally?"

Garrett interjected. "That will work well, but we won't take them into custody when they make the exchange. Don and Andrea will follow the money car and the rest of us will follow the drug car into town.

Nicole took the lead and drove to the same corner as yesterday. "

Sophie said into the phone, "We've got some business going on. A blue Toyota Camry, has pulled onto the road, License Plate Number SC85*7124."

Frank told her, "We'll follow you four car-lengths behind."

Garrett added, "Just remember that Don and Andrea will follow the money car."

"The rest of us will follow the car containing the new supply of drugs and as soon as the first transaction is in the works, we'll take them into custody."

Nicole stayed back as far as she could. She hid the car behind a tractor trailer in the right lane, moving to the middle lane long enough to see if the Camry was still in front of them.

Sophie realized they pulled onto the same service area. Nicole followed them and she and Sophie watched the exchange take place with a white Acura with SC tag number SC42*1436 but had no idea which way the trade went.

Garrett told Andrea and Don, "Keep an eye out for which ever car heads north."

The Acura pulled out first and headed north. Don said to everyone, "Andrea and I are on it."

Nicole followed the blue Camry with Sophie as her copilot, know that Frank and Garrett were somewhere behind them.

Don came on the phone to say, "We followed the car to the Hardrock Hotel Casino where Andrea went in to collect business cards and when she came back to the car, we watched as the two guys came out of the casino, got back into the Acura and drove south."

Garrett said into the phone, "That's a great job."

<>

Nicole stayed behind the Toyota a reasonable distance, traffic was light, so it was a fast-easy drive back to Baltimore. Nicole drove past the drug site. Sophie reported to Garrett, "The two guys from the Toyota and on the street dealing."

"Thanks Sophie, tell Nicole to drive past them; Frank and I are on it."

He and Frank took the two men into custody and put them into the back seat of the car while Garrett called for a tow truck to tow the blue Camry, license plate number SC85*7124 to the DEA's vehicle Forensic lab.

Buyers who were waiting to buy the drugs fled the scene in fear that they would also be taken into custody.

Sophie called Stacey, "There are two new bandits are in the Baltimore Detention Center."

Stacey asked, "Does anyone know how Andrea and Don did?"

"I don't believe that anyone has spoken with them yet."

"Sophie, do you think it would be a problem if I met with everyone for breakfast?"

"Not at all, we meet at Jimmy's in Fell's Point at 7:00."

"I'll be there."

Once the team did all it needed to do, everyone went home and watched the local news. The commentators announced, "Two new drug dealers were taken into custody by four unidentified federal agents."

Sophie missed the broadcast since she drove to the DEA Forensic lab where Garrett and Frank were waiting for her.

Sophie took fingerprints and found more than a trace of cocaine, indicating in her opinion that they were getting high during the drive back to Baltimore. She gave what she had to Garrett and he uncovered their names and criminal records, first was Gary Fawcett, 42 years-old with a prison record for Grand Auto Theft.

Sophie e-mailed Nicole what she and Garrett had uncovered and then went home.

<>

In the morning, the team met at Jimmy's in Fells Point. During breakfast, Stacey said, "I am so happy with the arrests you're making at the local level because they kept the buyers low and if you don't have buyers, you can't sell drugs, but we need to work our way up the food chain. I have Andrea and Don's report for the Hard Rock Casino and Hotel along with the business cards Andrea collected; however, we have no idea if those cards are real or fraudulent.

"I'm going to recommend that Joshua Albright and Sally Yarwood work undercover and report to Andrea York and Don Yarrow."

Andrea asked, "Will we need to get a room?"

"Yes, because I'm not sure how long it will take for this to play out. Joshua and Sally will work undercover as a married couple and stay in the same room in the Hardrock Casino and Hotel."

"Will Don and I need to stay in the same room?"

"No, I've made separate reservations for the two of you at the Showboat Casino and Hotel. Just make sure that you stay in close contact with Albright and Yarwood. Nicole, Sophie, Garrett and Frank, it's business as usual, and be sure to grab a few more dealers because I don't mind prosecuting them."

Nicole asked, "When will we get the chance to meet the two new members of the team?"

"It's likely that you'll never meet them because I don't want them compromised. We have a plant in the casino that is waiting who will work with them."

"Does anyone have questions?"

Garrett asked, "Can we drive up and visit?"

Stacey chuckled, as she said, "Maybe if you behave yourself."

Stacey paid the bill and after thanking her for breakfast the team left to do a day's work of keeping the lid on drug dealing.

Nicole drove to the corner where the dealers had been set up and no one was there, and nothing was going on.

Sophie said into the phone on her lap. "Garrett, there's no one here."

"Sophie, I'm not at all surprised, because we busted that site, so it's my guess that they moved to a new one, not far from their regular customers. Let split up and just cruise around and see what we can find."

They went in different directions. Garrett came on the phone and asked, "Haven't the dealers been using South Carolina car plates?"

"Yes, and it appears that their hot spot today is in front of the grocery at the corner of North Ave. and Asquith Street."

"Sophie, the dealers would stay close to their customers."

"Garrett, they're dealing right where I said they would on the sidewalk in front of a convenience store near the corner of Aisquith Street and E. Lafayette Avenue."

Frank said, "We'll be there in a few moments, so just sit tight."

Nicole pulled over north of the deal.

Sophie said, "Look as that VW Passat, that also has South Carolina Plates number SC72*5870."

Garrett and Frank lay low to make sure there were drug deals going down.

Frank said, "Nicole, they're on the move. Take the lead and we'll follow."

◇

Joshua Albright and Sally Yarwood kept pace with Andrea York and Don Yarrow, stopping at the same service center where they used the restrooms, grabbed cups of coffee, gassed up the cars and were back on the road.

When they reached Atlantic City, they waved goodbye.

Andrea and Don drove to the Showboat Hotel and Casino and checked in. They were delighted that they had a two-bedroom, suite two-bath suite. They were hungry so, they had lunch in the Guzzle and Grub in the hotel.

◇

Joshua and Sally went into the Hardrock hotel and used their under-cover names at the concierge's counter. "My name is Roger Shipley and I'm with my wife whose name is Sheila."

"We have a meeting with Mr. Rodriguez Hernández."

They were greeted by a middle-aged woman with graying brown hair wrapped in a French roll on the back of her head, dressed in a grey suit that fit her frame well.

"Mr. Hernandez is expecting you, so please follow me."

She tapped on his office door before opening it and said, "Mr. Hernandez your guests have arrived."

"My name is Roger Shipley, and this is my wife, Sheila."

"It's nice to meet you. Most folks just call me Rod. Stacey Greenwood recommended the two of you for a problem we're having in the casino with money laundering. I've been investigating this on my own and getting nowhere I installed surveillance cameras throughout the casino. I'm sure that the two of you are tired and hungry. There are menus in your room, get some lunch and rest, and then we'll get started tomorrow."

<>

After lunch in the Guzzle and Grub located in the hotel, Andrea and Don walked to Atlantic City's famous Steel Pier. It was cold and breezy, so they stopped in the Steel Pier Pub where they ordered coffee and dessert before making their way back to the hotel where they had a nightcap before calling it a day.

<>

Roger and Sheila had breakfast in Rod Hernández's suite. During breakfast Roger asked, "Rod, what makes you believe that the money is being laundered through the casino? Have you seen any evidence to support to support your thought?"

"Our accountant, Anthony Cain, has said that the numbers don't look correct."

"How so, what did he tell you?"

"Not much, but the process for the casino money, our bookkeeper, Janet Crawford works one day a week to tally up the week's casino money including its income and expenses. She writes a report and gives it to Cain."

"Are the reports she gives to Cain correct or is there a discrepancy?"

"Roger, I believe they are correct, because he checks them against the cash register tape and uses a simple tick and tie for the checking account."

"Rod, I know I'm repeating myself, but I have to ask why you're so sure that money is being laundered through the casino."

"Well I guess that when Cain told me that the numbers didn't look right, I assumed laundering was the reason."

"Rod, I'm not trying to be a smart ass, but did Cain give any details as to why the numbers didn't look correct?"

"No, as a matter of fact, he did not."

"I don't have enough information, so I'm not going to accuse the casino's accountant of any wrong-doing but see if you can meet with him and ask for details, so Sheila and I can do the job we were asked to do. While we're sitting here, have we been assigned to jobs?"

"Yes, you have been assigned to the position of security officer, which entails keeping an eye on everything going on, on the casino floor. Sheila, would you be able to work at the hotel concierge desk and record how payments are made, such as cash, check or credit cards?"

"Yes, I can do that"

Roger said, "Thanks for breakfast along with the meeting. We'll head out now and get to work."

They left his suite and walked to their job post.

After Sheila and Roger left, Rod Hernández called Anthony Cain to see if he was available for lunch.

"I sure am, so why don't we order lunch in my office at let's say noon."

<>

Sheila went down to the concierge where the woman sitting the desk asked, "How may I help you?"

"My name is Sheila Shipley and I need to collect information on the guest check-ins and the departures along with the name and room number along with payment method. Will that create a problem for you?"

"Not at all, my name is Lucy Crofton, please sit next to me. You can probably create a spreadsheet on the other computer."

<>

Roger walked the casino floor watching for anything that didn't look right. He kept a close eye on the Blackjack and Roulette tables watching where the dealers put the chips for the house. Pit Bosses came by regularly to collect the chips and delivered them to the cashier's office

<>

The morning was quiet, so Sheila put together a spreadsheet.

The guest traffic picked up 10:30 to around 11:00, as guests checked out. Sheila helped by shredding the used cardkeys.

<>

Rod Hernández met with Anthony Cain in Cain's office for lunch.

During lunch, Rod said, "Tony, the undercover agents are on site and asked me for more detail regarding your statement that the book didn't look quite right."

"Rod, I may have worded that statement wrong, because what I meant was that the casino made less the month before. How are they doing?"

"They just got started this morning but are very diligent folks who want to get to the bottom of the money laundering."

Unaware of the conversation between Rod and Cain, Roger wandered to the loading dock and watched. He wasn't surprised when the Mexican vendors arrived with full vegetable crates and left with dark bags that Roger assumed were full of money on; they're way back to Mexico, payment for the vegetables.

Roger made his way back into the casino wondering about those bags.

Quitting time arrived for Sheila and Roger.

Roger suggested that they have dinner outside of the casino so they could discuss the day.

Sheila called Andrea and asked to meet for dinner at the Guzzle and grub.

They sat at a table for four with Joshua and Sally (aka Roger and Sheila) and after ordering their beverages, Joshua said, "We need some advice because so far, we haven't uncovered a damn thing."

Andrea said, "I've had cases where the money is transferred from one casino to another one for laundering. Josh, there might not be any laundering going on in the Hard Rock."

"Andrea, I hear you, so what do we do now?"

"Keep your eyes open. I've seen two folks come inside together and one has a briefcase. When they leave the other one takes the briefcase. There are times when the transaction takes place on the parking lot. The best advice I can give you is to watch for a gym bag or a briefcase. Call if you see anything like that and we'll jump in and follow the car with the money."

Sally said, "Thanks for your help."

"It's not a problem; just remember to keep us in the loop."

Andrea paid the bill and Joshua and Sally walked in the chilly brisk air to the Hard Rock.

During the short walk, lapsing into his uncover name, Roger said, "We need to meet with Rod first thing in the morning."

Sheila asked, "Is it too late to call and ask to meet him over breakfast?

"No, it's not too late and we're almost to the hotel."

They made their way to their suite and Roger made the call, "Rod, is it possible for us to meet you for breakfast tomorrow morning?"

"Roger, I'm up and I don't want to wait until tomorrow to hear what you've learned. I'll meet you in the lobby bar."

Rod was waiting for them, "Drinks are on me."

Roger started the conversation, "We have two other folks here in Atlantic City. They're staying in the Showboat. Sheila and I had dinner with them earlier this evening. One is Andrea York who said that it's not likely the money is being laundered in the Hard Rock. It might only pass through to another location."

"What does that mean for us?"

"It means that no one in the Hard Rock is laundering money."

"Are you done here?"

"No, but we need to create a new strategy to watch for someone making a transfer, typically by a briefcase or a gym bag and then let our partners follow them."

"When will this start?"

"We start tomorrow."

Roger and Sheila were up early. Ordered breakfast sent to the room. Then showered and dressed and went down to the casino level, where Roger kept a close eye on the game tables along with the front door in ten-minute intervals and saw nothing that would cause concern, so he meandered over to the concierge counters and offered to get coffees for them. Sheila and Lucy said they would love one.

After delivering the coffees, he took a walk outside watching the traffic go by, telling himself that it wasn't likely that Rome was built in a day.

When their shift ended, Sheila called Andrea and asked if they could meet for dinner.

"Of course, we can meet here in the hotel in the ACE dining room."

By the time Roger and Sheila walked to the Showboat Roger and Sheila found them seated at a table for four.

After their beverages had been delivered, Andrea asked, "How did the day go?"

Roger spoke up to say, "There wasn't anything going on."

"Patience, Roger, Rome wasn't built in a day."

"That's what I've been telling myself all day."

"Roger, please don't get frustrated, because you might miss something if you do."

Andrea paid the tab and Roger and Sheila walked back to the Hard Rock and had a nightcap in the lobby.

Sheila asked, "How do you feel about what Andrea said?"

"I know she's right and I think I was just being overanxious. What about you?"

"I agree with you because I think, we both thought this wouldn't take long. Roger we need to go slow and not miss any details."

Roger signed the check and said to add it to the hotel bill. After which they went up to their suite to sleep.

Chapter Ten

Roger and Sheila kept to their routine breakfast in their suite, then showering and dressing before going down to the casino floor. They were early; the dealers hadn't arrived yet and neither had Lucy. The bar was open, so they sat together and had a cup of coffee talking about non-essential matter.

Roger asked, "Have you talked with your mother?"

"Yes, I did, I spoke with yesterday. Said Dad was doing fine,"

"That's great news."

"It really is, because we thought he was a goner."

They finished their coffees as the casino came to life. The slot machines were noisy when there was a payout, the card game 21 or bust tables were full of patrons as well with roulette and craps.

Roger thought to himself, if I were home, I'd be still in bed.

He then walked over to the concierge counter and asked, "Would you two ladies like a cup of coffee before the two of you are too busy to drink it?"

Both said they would, so he walked to the bar where a gentleman was sitting working on a laptop.

He asked, "Is the connection good?" While trying to get a peek at the computer screen

Just as he hit the send button, the gentleman said, "This casino has the best internet connection in all of Atlantic City."

He finished what he was doing, shut his computer down, put it in his bag, paid for his coffee and left through the front door.

Roger left the coffees sitting on the bar to try and at least get the car model along with the tag number. It was a late model Lexus; however, it was long gone before he could the whole tag number. The only thing he managed to get was the NY.

He called Andrea and told her what happened this morning.

She said, "Roger, your need to down because the transfer you watched may not be related to this case."

"But Andrea, its illegal, isn't it?"

"Yes, it is, so I'll check with Stacy to see if she wants to get involved with it."

"If she gives you an answer today, we can talk about it at dinner this evening."

"Yes, we can."

Roger returned to his job post of watching over the table while Sheila was helping Lucy check in by creating the card key

Roger and Sheila finished their shift and went up to their suite to shower, dress and walked to the Showboat to have dinner with Andrea and Don in the ACE Dining Room. Sheila and Roger took their seats at the table for four. The waiter took her beverage orders.

Roger was anxious, so before his beverage arrived, he asked Andrea, "Did you get in touch with Stacey?"

"Yes, I did, and let me tell you, she was impressed with what you uncovered with the man and his computer. She suggested that you and Sheila remain at the Hard Rock and if you see anyone at the bar that looks suspicious, call me and we'll take over. Would that work for you?"

"I don't have a problem with that, Andrea."

"I didn't think you would."

Now that that issue was resolved everyone had a pleasant dinner with lots of long tales creating laughter.

As Andrea asked for the bill, she said, "Don and I will come over under the guise of being tourists."

"Sheila and I would like that; it'll give you the chance to see how we work."

They walked back to the hotel and had a nightcap before going up to their room.

Sheila asked, "Are you sorry that Andrea and Don will take pick up this case to look for the launderer?"

"Nope."

With that said, they went up to their suite to go to bed.

◇

In the morning Sheila and Roger took breakfast in their suite.

During breakfast, Roger said, "We need to meet with Rod and give him an update."

Roger called Rod and asked he and Sheila could meet with him?

"Of course, we can meet. I'm available now. If that works for you, I'm okay with it."

They met in Rod's office.

Roger explained how he saw a man sitting at the bar transferring money and he assumed it was offshore He said two more folks were to follow the trail. Sheila and I are going to stay here with your permission of course and feed info to the other team.

"That is great news to me, because as much as we trusted the staff, there was a small margin of doubt. Of course, you may continue to stay here and continue your work."

They went down to the casino floor and separated to do go to the worksites.

Since it was so early, they went to the bar to enjoy a fresh cup of coffee before the action started.

◇

In Baltimore, Nicole Sophie, Garrett, and Frank took dealers into custody daily. It was apparent that the local dealers bought the drugs out of state, but the Baltimore Team didn't worry about that because the other half of the team was working in New Jersey. The bandits were able to buy a large supply with just a 20% of what they brought to the transfer spot.

The dealers moved regularly to a new location but stayed close to their regular customers, but the agents always managed to find them and took them and whatever money and cocaine they had into custody.

Stacey Greenwood would meet with them on Monday morning for breakfast to update them with anything new and to listen to them making sure they had everything they needed. On this particular Monday morning, she reported to them, "US Attorney Chennault is overly impressed with your work. There are now four judges assigned to this case, so that means that the four of you will need to take time out of your busy schedules to testify in court. The judges are planning to schedule one day a week for this case."

Each Monday, Nicole asked, "How's the team in New Jersey doing?"

To answer her, each Monday, they met, Stacey always said, "They're doing fine."

That didn't give the Baltimore team much information to know how it was really going.

◇

Back in the Hard Rock, activity started to pick up and the casino floor was active with the sound of the slot machines. Sheila and Lucy were preparing for the onslaught of guests checking out by 11:00 am and would take advantage of the quiet before the check-in guests started.

Out of the corner of her eye, Sheila watched the same guy sit at the bar, order coffee and then opened his laptop.

Roger nodded to her that he saw it and left the bar to call Andrea, "He's here at the bar."

"We're on our way."

Roger watched as they entered the casino and head to the slot machines where they could see him at them at the bar.

When that was does done, Andrea and Don followed him out the door leaving Roger in the casino without an update.

Roger went back to walking the floor knowing the nothing was taking place.

When their shift ended, they went to their suite to shower and change.

They were surprised when Roger's cell phone rang, "Andrea was calling to make sure they were up for dinner in the ACE restaurant in the Showboat.

Roger said, "We'll be there."

Andrea and Don were seated at a table for four when they arrived.

After the beverages arrived, Andrea said, "His name is Pablo Castaneda. We confiscated his computer and two Deputy US Marshals are transporting him to the Baltimore City Detention Center. While I had his computer, I learned that he was transferring funds to offshore accounts for three different US Citizens, please don't fall off your chairs when I tell you who they are. The first is Craig Morton, owner of Morton Investments, the second one is Jack Bagley, and owner of Bagley Real Estate and the last one is Joseph, owner of Barns Yachts."

Roger said, "Andrea, that's but none of those names are related to our drug case, are they?"

"Roger don't jump to any assumptions, because all three of them were a large part of this case. They made a ton of money by financing drug dealers."

"Andrea, are you saying that it happened in our back yard?"

"Yes, that's what I'm saying, but let me continue to say that I believe that was part of the plan; to make sure we were kept off the trail."

"In that case, Sheila and I would like to congratulate you and Don for a successful case."

Don said, "If you hadn't tipped us off, we couldn't have uncovered what we did."

Before everyone left the restaurant, Sheila asked, "Is this it, the end of our going undercover and go home?"

"Yes, it does."

Andrea paid the dinner tab, so Roger and Sheila walked to the Hard Rock and had a nightcap at the lobby bar.

Roger said, "We'll need to meet with Rod in the morning and update him."

<>

After Breakfast, Roger called Rod, "Sheila and I would like to meet with you."

"In that case, come on up to my office before the casino floor gets busy."

When they arrived in his office, Rod asked, "Can I order you both a cup of coffee?"

They thanked him, but said they had just finished breakfast

Roger started the conversation, "Rod, there was no money laundering in the hotel or casino, that one guy, who was using the hotel's internet at bar to transfer money to offshore accounts for several US citizens, which means that our job in your casino is done."

Rod asked, "Are you planning to check out today?"

Sheila nodded her head as she said, "Yes, we are."

Rod said, "Before you go, can you tell your real names?"

Roger said, "My name is Joshua Albright" and Sheila said, "My name Sally Yarwood."

"The two of you are always welcome to the Hard Rock on my tab."

They thanked him and then went to their suite to grab their clothes and then went to the concierge desk to check out using their undercover names.

Lucy told Sheila, "I'm really going to miss you."

"Lucy, I had fun working with you."

They went out the door, to start the drive back to Maryland. Once they were headed south, Sally called Stacey Greenwood to let her know they were on their way home.

Stacey said, "We're still doing the Monday morning breakfast at Jimmy's at 7:00."

Sally said, "Josh and I will be there."

Josh dropped Sally off at her house in Fells Point, as she started to get out of the car, he asked, "What are your plans for the weekend?"

She answered. "Sleep."

He said, "That's a great idea."

Josh then drove to his home in Glen Arm, took a shower and went to bed.

Josh and Sally took the weekend off to lay low with reading and napping since Monday would arrive soon enough.

<>

Sally and Josh arrived at Jimmy's at the same time. They said good morning to one another and then went into the restaurant to find folks rearranging tables to accommodate 9 people.

Once every sat, Stacy Greenwood said, "We may to find a larger breakfast meeting location. We have two members you may not know, Sally Yarwood and Joshua Albright. They worked undercover at the Hard Rock Casino and Hotel, to uncover money laundering. They met Andrea and Don every evening for dinner in the ACE Restaurant in the Showboat Hotel and Casino to update Andrea and Don. Jose kept his eye on a man sitting at the bar using his laptop to transfer funds to offshore accounts. He contacted Andrea and she and Don uncovered the name of the man, his name is Pablo Castaneda, who was laundering money for three US citizens.

"The first is Craig Morton, owner of Morton Investments. The second is Jack Bagley, owner of Bagley Real Estate. The last on is Joseph Barnes, owner of Barnes Yachts."

She gave everyone a chance to digest what she'd just said before moving on to the Baltimore Team.

"The Baltimore team consisting of Nicole, Sophie, Garrett and Frank took in custody 30 drug dealers along with six kilos of cocaine and six million dollars in cash."

Stacey gave everyone a moment to absorb what she just said. She went on to say, "Judge Gerald Chaney would hear the money laundering cases separately starting with Pablo Castaneda. I'll notify everyone as soon as I get the dates."

Everyone thanked her for breakfast and updating them on the case, before leaving Jimmy's.

Everyone on Greenwood's team laid low and enjoyed the quiet.

Sophie called Helen and Fred to give them an update on where the case moved to. "Patrick and Simmons were in transit to the US District Court when the car was attacked. They ended up in the hospital for at least a month and they are in the Witness Protection Program."

Fred said rather angrily, "Sophie, does that mean they will not serve the sentence that the Judge in Crisfield gave them?"

"Fred, I know that sounds wrong, but they led us to a bigger fish and the Federal Judge in Baltimore said they would be murdered in prison."

"Sophie, don't try to soft toe this, they murdered our daughter and son-in-law and now they won't serve a sentence for it?"

She felt like whale dung when she said, "That's right, but living in WITSEC is no party. They were under surveillance 24 hours a day."

"Like I give a shit." He then slammed the phone down cutting off their call, which made her feel worse.

After the call she had with Fred Barton, she wasn't sure if she should call Tim Willoughby in Crisfield, but she made the call.

He answered on the first ring and said, "I thought you dumped me."

"You know I wouldn't do that. The two kids were heading to the Federal Courthouse and the car was attacked and that sent them to the hospital. Their attorney Antonio De Luca was shot dead in the middle of the street. Patrick and Simms were put in the WITSEC program. However, that small drug case on them, let us to bigger fish in the pond for money laundering."

"It's no wonder that you haven't had time to call me."

<>

During the next Monday's breakfast meeting, Stacey announced the arraignment schedules have been set. "Pablo Castaneda is set for arraignment for this Thursday at 9:00 am before Judge Gerald Chaney. Craig Morton is scheduled on Friday at 9:00 am. Jack Bagley is scheduled for Monday at 9:00 am and Joseph Barnes for Tuesday at 9:00 am. Their attorney is Charlene Bradford and she has a great reputation for getting her clients off with an acquittal, so we're gonna need to work hard.

Stacy paid the tab and the team left to go home until Thursday.

Stacy met with Charlene Bradford in Stacy's office to give her what she had for evidence along with her witness's name, Andrea York."

Bradford thanked her and with a cocky tone said, "I wish you luck in the courtroom."

Greenwood was pissed, so she said, "Ms. Bradford, I wish you luck as well."

Bradford left her office saying, "I will see you on Thursday morning for the arraignment before Judge Chaney." She then, left Greenwood's office, slamming the door behind her.

Greenwood had been really pissed when Bradford was in her office but chuckled now at the memory of Bradford stomping out of her office and slamming the door behind her.

Stacy finished out her day and went home to relax in her sunroom with a glass of wine.

The week flew by and before she knew it, it was Thursday, so she grabbed a cup of coffee, jumped into the shower, and dressed. She then made her way to the courthouse to find that the courtroom doors were still locked. She sat on a bench in the hall to review her notes for this morning's arraignment for Pablo Castaneda.

Stacey was more than surprised when Bradford sat beside her.

Bradford justified her sitting next to Greenwood by saying, "This is the only bench on this hall."

The look on Bradford's face was priceless, when Greenwood's team of eight joined her in her in that hall.

Pablo Castaneda sauntered down the looking as though he was the man in charge and knew it. When he saw the crowd in the hall, he stopped and stood where he was, posing for what he believed were folks of the media waiting to enter the courtroom to hear the judge release him on his own recognizance.

The bailiff unlocked the courtroom doors to let them in.

Bradford walked with her client, Pablo Castaneda to the defense table.

Castaneda turned to watch Greenwood walk to the prosecutor's table and what he had believe were member of the media were in fact members of the prosecutor's team. Who filled the two rows behind the prosecutor's table, so in his mind it was too many people on her team to watch the Judge release him on his personal recognizance and for the first time he was nervous about what the results would be, in terms of bail.

The bailiff entered the courtroom, through a side door to call out "Hear-Ye. Hear-Ye All rise as The Honorable Gerald Chaney enters the courtroom for, he arraignment of Pablo Castaneda, defendant in case number 17-5240, for Money Laundering in violation of Title 18 USC § 1957."

Once he was sitting on the bench, Judge Chaney asked, "Will everyone please be seated."

He then asked the defendant to stand. Bradford stood with her client.

Judge Chaney then asked, "Mr. Castaneda, how do you plea?"

"Not guilty, Your Honor."

"Your plea is duly noted, and you may sit with your attorney."

Chaney asked, "Does the Government have a recommendation as to bail?"

Greenwood stood to address the judge, "Yes Your Honor, it does. The Government sees the defendant as a flight risk, so our recommendation us that the defendant be held without the benefit of bail."

Bradford jumped up from her chair and stood ramrod straight as she faced the judge, "Your Honor, my client has an established business and a family in the US, so I do not believe he's a flight risk and request that he be released on his own recognizance."

"Counselor, thank you for input, but the defendant will remain in custody."

"Will everyone please remain in the courtroom? I'm going to create a concise schedule for this working with my court clerk. We have it reads; counselors will receive the schedule electronically,

Craig Morton will be arraigned tomorrow, Friday March 3 at 9:00 before this bench.

The Probable Cause Hearing for Pablo Castaneda at 1:30 pm on the same day.

Jack Bagley will appear before this court on Monday March 6 at 9:00 for his arraignment

The Probable Cause Hearing for Craig Morton will follow at 1:30 pm on the same day

Joseph Barns is scheduled for his arraignment before this court on Tuesday March 7, at 9:00

Jack Bagley will appear before this court at 1:30 for his Probable cause hearing

Joseph Barns is scheduled for his Probable Cause
Hearing on Wednesday. March 8, at 9:00

I'm quite sure there will be modifications to this schedule. Are there questions before I adjourn today?"

There were none, so he banged his gavel as he announced, "This court is adjourned"

The media flew out of the court room to make the 5:00 news

Excitement grew during breakfast because they had worked hard on this case and wanted to be a part of its end.

Andrea said, "I hope that we nail them to the wall because they are arrogant bastards."

No one at the table had ever heard Andrea say anything profane, but they had to agree with her.

Nicole paid the breakfast tab with a healthy tip since they would be coming here for breakfast for a long time to come.

They drove separately and parked in the garage on Lombard Street from the Courthouse, and then gathered as a team to walk to the courthouse,

After going through the security checkpoint in the lobby, they made their way to the 7th floor where they found Greenwood, Bradford and her client Craig Morton, who was dressed in a very expensive business suit, but looked green around the gills because he knew that Pablo Hernandez was in the courthouse lock up waiting for his probable cause hearing later today.

The bailiff opened the courtroom door and in they went. Craig Morton walked into the courtroom with his attorney, Charlene Bradford, to sit at the defense table. Once he was seated, he turned around to watch the prosecutor walk to her table with her team right behind her, to sit on the bench behind her. He then focused on the media and citizens find seats, to watch the arraignment.

His stomach turned over when he saw the media, because if his clients ended up seeing this in either the newspaper or on the local news, his career was over.

The Bailiff entered through a side door to call out, "Hear-Ye, Hear-Ye. All rise as the Honorable Gerald Chaney enters the courtroom for the arraignment of Craig Morton, defendant, in case number 17-3241, charged with Money Laundering in violation of Title 18 USC § 1957.

When Judge Chaney sat on the bench, he asked everyone to please sit.

He then asked, "Will the defendant, Craig Morton, please stand."

His attorney, Charlene Bradford stood with her client.

Judge Chaney asked the defendant, "Mr. Morton, how do you plead?"

Morton knew his knees were knocking when he said, "Not guilty, Your Honor."

"Duly noted, you may sit."

Judge Chaney then asked, "Does the Government have a recommendation for bail?"

"Yes, Your Honor, it does, the Government feels the defendant Craig Morton is a flight risk and recommend that the defendant be held without the benefit of posting bail.

"So noted Counselor, the defendant is remanded to the Baltimore City Detention Center without the benefit of posting bail."

The judge called for a one-hour recess before the Probable Cause hearing for Pablo Castaneda.

While waiting for Pablo Castaneda's Probable Cause Hearing, Bradford sat in the court lock-up with her client. Her client behaved arrogantly saying that he didn't deserve this treatment, and someone was going to pay for it

Bradford did her best to settle him down and he would have none of it, swearing that someone was going to pay with his or her life.

The bailiff came to the lockup to retrieve the defendant and his attorney and walked with them to the defense table.

Greenwood and her team had taken restroom breaks.

The bailiff entered the courtroom to call out "Hear-Ye, Hear-Ye. All rise as the Honorable Gerald Chaney enters the courtroom for the Probable Cause Hearing of Pablo Castaneda in case number 17-5240, for Money Laundering in violation of Title 18 USC § 1957."

Once he was seated on the bench, he said, "Please be seated. The Government may proceed with the Probable Cause for this case.

"Thank you, Your Honor. The Government has evidence to present to show that the defendant, Pablo Castaneda, laundering for three US Citizens. The first is Craig Morton, owner of Morton Investments. The second is Jack Bagley, owner of Bagley Real Estate. The last person is Joseph Barnes, the owner of Barnes Yachts. The evidence will be supported by a witness."

"Thank you, counselor, the Government has met its Probable cause requirements."

Judge Chaney turned to face Bradford, "How does the defense wish this case to be heard? Counselor, do you want this case heard by a jury or by me?"

Bradford stood to say, "Your Honor, the defense wishes to be heard before a jury."

Chaney conferred with his court clerk and then announced, "The jury selection is scheduled to Monday April 3 at 9:00 am and trial for Tuesday April 4 at 9: am. Notices will be sent to counsel. This Court is adjourned; however, I suspect that I will see everyone in the morning for Craig Morton's Probable Hearing. This Court is adjourned."

Greenwood's team waited for the courtroom to clear before getting their cars to drive to the Thames Street Oyster House where they took up the entire bar. They were exuberant with the pride the pride they felt with being on the winning team

Nicole said to Andrea, "If it hadn't been for you, we'd still be chasing small time deals in Baltimore City.

Andrea said, "Those small-time deals led us to this case, and everyone was a part of it."

Nicole paid the tab and said, "I'll see everyone at Jimmy's, no later than 7:30 tomorrow morning.

Everyone left the restaurant to drive home carrying a glow of success around each one.

Some read, some watched the television and some just went to bed.

They had the weekend off.

<>

The team met at Jimmy's for breakfast on Monday morning and chatted about the upcoming day's activities. The furniture store owner is being arraigned this morning. Nicole said and then that is it for the day.

Sophie said, "We'll be back to the routine tomorrow of an arraignment in the morning and a probable cause in the afternoon."

Nicole paid the tab for breakfast and everyone made their way to the parking garage and they walked together to the courthouse, through the security and then an elevator to the 7th floor. Stacy was there, sitting on the bench. After a round of good morning,

Greenwood and her team followed them, with Greenwood sitting at the Prosecutor's table and her team sat on the first bench behind her.

The bailiff entered the courtroom and called out. "Hear-Ye, Hear-Ye. All rise as the Honorable Gerald Chaney enters the courtroom for the Probable Cause hearing of Craig Morton in case number 17-5241, for Money Laundering in violation of Title 18 USC § 1957"

Judge Chaney asked, "Will everyone please sit"

The Judge said, "The Government may proceed with its probable cause."

Thank you, Your Honor. The Government has evidence to present to show that the defendant, Jack Bagley was involved in laundering with Pablo Castaneda.

Judge Chaney said, "The Government has met the probable requirements. Does the defense have a recommendation as to jury or heard by the court?"

"Your Honor, we prefer to be heard by a Jury."

Chaney conferred with his courtroom clerk.

He then announced, "Jury selection is scheduled for Monday March 13, at 9:00 am and the trial will begin on Tuesday, March 14, at 9:00 am

The bailiff came into courtroom from a side door and called out, "Hear-Ye, Hear-Ye. All rise as the Honorable Gerald Chaney enters the courtroom for the arraignment of Jack Bagley in case number 17-5242, for Money Laundering in violation of Title 18 USC § 1957"

Judge Chaney sat on the bench, he asked, "Will everyone please be seated."

He then asked the defendant to please stand. Bradford stood as well.

"Mr. Bagley, how do you plead?"

"Not guilty, Your Honor."

"Duly noted. Does the Government have a recommendation as to bail?"

Greenwood stood, "Your Honor, the Government believes that the defendant is a flight risk and recommends that he be held without the benefit of bail."

The Judge said, "The defendant will be remanded to the Baltimore City Jail."

This court is now adjourned.

The media fled from the courtroom.

Stacey walked with them to the parking garage. Nicole said, "I didn't think that Bradford looked well today."

"Nicole, she has a full plate."

"Stacey, you have a full plate of your own. I just don't want her to go the way De Luca went."

"Neither do I. I'll see you in the morning."

Everyone went home remembering Antonio De Luca being shot down in the middle of Lombard Street.

He checked with his clerk and then said, we'll "Schedule this case for jury selection on Monday, April 10 at 9:00 am and trial on Tuesday, April 11, at 9:00 am."

The Judge said, "I will hear Probable Cause for Joseph Barnes tomorrow at 9:00 am."

The media fled from the courtroom to get on the 5:00 news shows that only one more hearing is to be heard tomorrow morning and then they will report the trials.

Greenwood's team met at the Rusty Scupper to talk about the trials, "I have no doubt that Joseph Barnes's probable cause will turn into a trial. I've never worked with anyone as determined as this team to get the job done."

Stacey paid the tab, but before leaving, Nicole said, "Breakfast at Jimmy's no later than 7:30."

Everyone went home extremely excited that tomorrow would be the last of this phase and on to the trials.

<>

On Tuesday morning the team met at Jimmy's for breakfast, Nicole paid the tab. Everyone used their personal car to the parking lot and then walked together to the court and they walked single file through the security check point. The bailiff unlocked the courtroom doors, and everyone entered taking their seats. The media followed them in looking for the best bench to watch the arraignment from.

The bailiff entered the courtroom from a side door and called out, "Hear-Ye, Hear-Ye. All rise as the Honorable Gerald Chaney enters the courtroom for the arraignment of Joseph Barnes in case number 17-5243, for Money Laundering in violation of Title 18 USC § 1957."

When Judge Chaney sat, he said, "Please sit."

He then asked the defendant to stand.

Bradford stood with her client.

The Judge asked the defendant, "How do you plead?"

With a confident voice, Bagley said, "Not guilty Your Honor."

Judge Chaney said, "Duly noted."

"Does the Government have a recommendation as to bail?"

"Yes, your honor, it does. We see the defendant as a flight risk and held without the benefit of bail."

Judge Chaney said, "The defendant will be remanded to the Baltimore City Detention Center."

He then banged his gavel as the Judge announce, "This Court will take a one-hour recess."

The bailiff went to the court lockup to retrieve Bradford and her client.

Once they were seated at the defense table, the bailiff left and the returned to the courtroom, through the side door, and called out, "Hear-Ye, Hear-Ye. All rise as the Honorable Gerald Chaney enters the courtroom for the probable cause hearing of Jack Bagley in case number 17-5142, for Money Laundering in violation of Title 18 USC § 1957."

Greenwood stood to present her probable cause to the judge, "Thank you, Your Honor. The Government has evidence to present to show that the defendant, Jack Bagley was involved in laundering with **Pablo Castaneda**"

The judge announced, "The Government has met the Probable cause regulations."

"Ms. Bradford how does the defense wish to be heard?"

"By a jury, Your Honor."

He checked with his clerk and then said, "We'll schedule this case for jury selection on Monday, April 10 at 9:00 am and trial on Tuesday, April 11, at 9:00 am.

The Judge said, "I will hear Probable Cause for Joseph tomorrow at 9:00 am."

The media fled from the courtroom to get on the 5:00 news shows that only one more hearing is to be heard tomorrow morning and then they will report the trials.

Greenwood's team met at the Rusty Scupper to talk about the trials, "I have no doubt that Joseph Barnes's probable cause will turn into a trial. I've never worked with anyone as determined as this team to get the job done."

Stacey paid the tab, but before leaving, Nicole said, "Breakfast at Jimmy's no later than 7:30."

Everyone went home overly excited that tomorrow would be the last of this phase and on to the trials.

<>

On Wednesday morning, everyone met at Jimmy's for breakfast at 7:30. Sophie said it's gonna be a while before we have breakfast together.

Nicole paid the tab and they drove separately to the garage across from the courthouse. Just like every other day, they walked together to the courthouse, through the security check point and up the elevator to the 7th floor.

Greenwood sat alone on the bench in front of the courtroom doors. She explained that Charlene Bradford is in the court's lockup with her client.

The bailiff came into the hall to unlock the courtroom doors.

Stacey and her team entered the courtroom knowing there was a flood of media along with interested citizens.

The bailiff brought Bradford and her client in the courtroom and they sat at the defense table.

In Stacey's opinion, Charlene look like death had taken her and thought about what Nicole had said about De Luca.

The bailiff came through the side door to call out, "Hear-Ye, Hear-Ye. All rise as the Honorable Gerald Chaney enters the courtroom for the probable cause hearing of Joseph Barns in case number 17-5143, for Money Laundering in violation of Title 18 USC § 1957."

Judge Chaney said. "The Government may proceed."

Greenwood stood to present her probable cause to the judge, "Thank you, Your Honor. The Government has evidence to present to show that the defendant, Joseph Barns was involved in laundering with **Pablo Castaneda**"

"Thank you, does the defense give a recommendation as trial by jury or trial by the bench?"

"Yes, Your Honor, it does. We would prefer a jury trial."

Chaney checked with his court clerk and then announced, Jury selection will be scheduled for Monday, April 17, at 9:00 am and trial on Tuesday April 18 at 9:00 am. All counselors will be notified of the dates and times.

Judge Chaney banged his gavel as he announced, "This court is now adjourned."

Greenwood and her team waited while the crowd left the courtroom, before asking them if they wanted to meet at Joyce James for drinks and appetizers. The team chattered over the victory.

Stacey put a damper on the celebration when she said, "Now is a good time to celebrate what we've achieve this far, but the trial could be a ball buster against four businessmen. Juries can difficult at times, acquitting a defendant when we know that he's guilty. I did not intend to be a party-pooper; I just wanted to let you know what's ahead of us. You're a great team and I'll try hard not to get an acquittal for any of them. I'll send e-mails when I hear anything useful including jury selection and trial date reminders.

Greenwood paid the tab and told them again, "I will keep everyone informed and am ready, willing, and able to answer any questions.

Chapter Eleven

The night before the jury selection, Greenwood created a list of the defendants with their court dates and sent it to her team via e-mail

Her team sent e-mails thanking her for the chart. Since they were technically still in March everyone took the time to do some housekeeping, go to the grocery store and had time to eat the food before it went moldy. They met with their bosses to update them.

Sophie's boss, Joe Schofield told her, "Sophie I had to hire someone to fill your position at least until you came to me to reclaim your job."

"Joe, that's okay because now I know that I had a job that meant something."

"Sophie, you created that job and turned it into something useful."

Joe said, "Thank you for that compliment."

They met twice for dinner at the Thames Street Oyster House and enjoyed not only the food and drink, but the friendships that were developing. The made bets on how long each trial would run.

They continued to meet on Monday Morning and on Monday, April 3. Nicole said, "According to the chart Stacey sent us she and Bradford are in the process of selecting a jury for the Pablo Castaneda case and if they match, we'll be able to watch the trial."

Andrea said, "I have to sit in the hall until I'm called in to testify."

Sophie said, "Wouldn't you like to be a fly on the courtroom wall?"

Nicole agreed with Sophie and paid the breakfast tab.

Everyone went home to wait for the call.

<>

In the courtroom, Judge Chaney addressed the 25 folks sitting in his courtroom, "I am to see you here doing your civic duty. The Clerk's office gave you each a card with a number on it. The attorney's sitting in front of my bench will address you by your card number. The goal for the attorneys is to agree on fourteen jurors. Twelve will make up the jury, the two alternative jurors. The alternative juror will fill the spot, if another juror is unable to serve, the alternate step in. The attorneys will alternate in calling out numbers. Once a number is called, they each can question that number.

Judge Chaney said, "The Government may call a number."

Greenwood stood and looked at the potential jurors, with only a number to go by, it was a crap shoot. She called for number 19 a stately older gentleman stood.

She called out, "Will Number 19 please stand?"

A stately older gentleman stood.

"Do you work?"

"No ma'am I retired thirty years ago from an accounting firm."

In her mind, Stacey know Bradford was going to vote no for number 19

As Greenwood went to sit in her chair, Bradford stood and asked him, "Do you do any accounting on the side?"

"If you count that I still the tax returns free for my family, then yes, I do accounting, on the side."

Greenwood knew that Bradford would never vote for this gentleman and that was a shame, he'd make a great jury member for her.

Bradford returned to her chair with a smirk on her face.

That's how they worked, alternating from the Government to the Defense until Judge Chaney called for lunch.

"Judge Chaney told the prospective jurors' lunch is in the jury room, the bailiff will escort you there. I'm going to ask that you not discuss anything about this case or who may or may not be selected. The attorneys will join me for lunch in my chambers."

In his Chambers, Judge Chaney said, "The two of you match on all, but number 12."

After lunch everyone returned to the courtroom and using the same method of alternating questions between the Government and the defense, they had a jury by 4:00 in the afternoon.

Greenwood and Bradford waited quietly in the courtroom, while the bailiff took the jurors to the jury room, followed by Judge Chaney, who called out the numbers that were selected as voting jurors and the two alternatives. The numbers not chosen for this case can collect their checks from the Clerk's Office, with my thanks.

He then went on to say, "The twelve of you need to elect a foreman or a forewoman who will submit any questions or issues to the bailiff, who will be standing outside of the door and will bring them to me. I also want to make sure that you understand that you may not discuss this case with anyone; if you do, I'll have to dismiss you from the jury and have an alternate take your place. One last thing, there's a caterer on standby to bring you dinner.

Greenwood and Bradford went to wait with Judge Chaney and just after 7:00 the bailiff brought a note to the judge that the jury had a foreman.

The Judge told Greenwood and Bradford, "Go on home and get some rest, because we have a trial tomorrow."

As they were leaving the courthouse, Greenwood told Bradford, "We were chasing drug money and Agent Andrea York found it and that's where the laundering charge came from, they were profits on the drugs.

"Stacey, I wish I could tell you I'm surprised, but I'm not."

"I just wanted you to know before we get in the courtroom tomorrow."

"I appreciate that."

Greenwood created a conference call to let her team know that Pablo Castaneda's trial will begin tomorrow at 9:00 am.

<>

On Tuesday, April 4, at 7:30 am, Stacey's team met for breakfast at Jimmy's.

During breakfast, Sophie asked, "What happens to the case if by some strange reason Castaneda is acquitted?"

Nicole told her, "The trials for everyone else will continue on and that's reason Judge is hearing them separately."

Sophie said, "I understand and that makes sense."

Nicole paid the breakfast tab and they drove separately to the parking garage and then met on the sidewalk to make their way to the courthouse as a team. They went single file through the security checkpoint, and then took the elevator to the 7th floor.

Stacy smiled as she watched them step off the elevator.

The bailiff unlocked the courtroom doors and there was media created a stampede to get into the courtroom first.

The bailiff winked at Greenwood's team as they entered the courtroom to find that the bailiff had roped off the bench behind Greenwood.

The media went wild when Pablo Castaneda and his attorney entered the courtroom through the side door. They stood and pushed their colleagues aside to get a better look.

Sophie leaned over to whisper to Nicole. "It looks like he was roughed up in the detention center."

Nicole whispered back, "It looks to me that someone beat the shit out of him."

The bailiff came through the side door with the jurors in tow and once they were seated in the jury box the bailiff left and returned to call out, out "Hear-Ye, Hear-Ye. All rise as the Honorable Gerald Chaney enters the courtroom for the trial of Pablo Castaneda in case number 17-5240, for Money Laundering in violation of Title 18 USC § 1957"

When Chaney sat on the bench, he saw the media ready to cover this trial, like sharks circling a life raft eager for someone to fall in and become dinner.

Chaney asked everyone to please sit.

He then asked, "Is the Government prepared to make its Opening Statement?"

"Yes, Your Honor it is."

Greenwood stood and then went to stand at the defense table. "What you see sitting at the defense table is a well-dressed gentleman, wearing a Giorgio Amani suit valued at close to $7,000.00. Mr. Castaneda must be very successful in his business. The Government will show the jury beyond a reasonable doubt that the defendant is laundering drug profits for not only himself, but for three businessmen as well. I assure you after the testimony supporting the evidence; you will have no choice other than to vote guilty."

"Thank you, Your Honor, the Government has concluded its Opening Summary.

"Thank you, counselor. The defense may proceed to its Opening Summary."

"Thank you, Your Honor.

Bradford stood to address the jury. "I believe the Government was more focused on what my client was wearing rather than any crime he may have committed. Being successful in business, successful enough to purchase an expensive suit is not a criminal offense. I hear a number of holes in the Government's Opening

Summary that created doubt in my mind and if you agree, you must vote for an acquittal"

Thank you, Your Honor the defense has completed its Opening Summary"

Judge Chaney called for a fifteen minute recess before the Government calls its witness to the stand. No one left the courtroom even though some folks looked as though they need to/

When Chaney returned to the bench, the bailiff called out "Hear-Ye, Hear-Ye. All rise as the Honorable Gerald Chaney enters the courtroom for the trial of Pablo Castaneda in case number 17-5240, for Money Laundering in violation of Title 18 USC § 1957"

Greenwood thought that Castaneda looked cocky as he stood with Bradford

When Judge Chaney took his seat on the bench, he asked everyone to please sit and once everyone was sitting, he said, "The Government may call for its witness to take the stand."

Greenwood stood and called for Andrea York.

The bailiff retrieved her from the hall and as he swore her in, Greenwood pulled the evidence from her briefcase.

She then approached the witness and asked her to state her full name for the record.

Greenwood smiled as Andrea confidently said, "Andrea Lynn York."

"Ms. York, are you currently employed?"

"Yes, ma'am I am. I'm a Drug Enforcement Agent. I am responsible for cataloging all incoming drugs and money. It is also my responsibility to investigate the origin of the money and where it goes."

Greenwood walked York's report to Bradford first and then to the witness stand.

"Ms. York, did you write this report?"

"Yes ma'am, I did."

"Can you explain what this report says to the jury?"

York's confident voice soothed the jurors. "This report says that Off-Shore banking is not illegal as long as the US taxes are paid. In this case, the money was sent off-shore from the drug selling profits without being taxed. In this country, profiting from selling drugs is very much a criminal offense typically referred to as money laundering."

Judge Chaney asked, "Would the defense like to cross examine this witness?"

Bradford knew she was going down and was probably going to become fish food in some hidden river, but was gonna go down with some gusto.

She stood and said, "Yes, Your Honor, I would welcome the opportunity to question the witness."

Bradford stood and then walked to stand to face the witness. "Ms. York, please explain to the jury and me how and why you are so sure that my client was involved with the sale of drugs?"

"I was part of a team. We started watching the street corner dealers in Baltimore City exchange money for drugs through the window of his car. We followed the car to Atlantic City and checked into separate hotels. Two of the folks worked uncover in the targeted casino. They watched as the defendant sat at the casino's bar while he transferred money to off-shore accounts."

"Ms. York, I believe that you are aware that sending to off-shore banks isn't illegal."

"It is when the money was received from drug sales."

"Your Honor, I have no more questions for this witness."

Judge Chaney announced a fifteen break before moving onto closing arguments. No one left the courtroom, so the Judge said, "The Government may proceed to its closing argument."

Greenwood stood and walked to the jury. The folks sitting in the courtroom were so quiet that the only thing anyone could hear was the sound of her six-inch stiletto heels as she walked across the hardwood floor. All eyes in the courtroom including Judge Chaney watched her hips swayed in rhythm to her strut.

When she reached her destination she stated with a confident voice, "The details of this case may have sounded complicated during the trial; however, they were not. This was a simple case of a well-dressed business man, who became greedy and gained his wealth and power through drug trafficking and then had the audacity to send that money to an off-shore to avoid paying taxes, while the average citizen, like you and me would be sent to jail for not paying our taxes. If you agree with me, you must vote guilty."

As she walked back to the prosecutor's table, she said, Your Honor, the Government has concluded its closing summation.

"Thank you, counselor. The defense may move forward.

When defense counsel Charlene Bradford stood to address the jury, she smirked at Greenwood as she passed the Prosecutor's table on her way to the jury box. With a soft alluring voice she addressed the jury members. "The Government clearly defamed my client to get a guilty verdict from you. My client was the product of a poor Mexican family who were murdered in their home while my client was out helping other children with their school work. He made a name for himself and helped other children find jobs. Yes, he's wearing a very expensive suit and yes he's become an excellent businessman and putting money into the pockets of the less fortunate."

Everyone was focused on the juror's faces and saw that they didn't believe one word Bradford said.

Judge Chaney asked the bailiff to take the jury into the jury room and he would be in shortly.

When he entered the jury room, he asked, "By a show of hands, do the members of the jury wish to continue today?"

Everyone in the room raised a hand.

"In that case, let me lead your through the process. You will need to appoint a foreman or forewoman who will represent you. Any and all questions will be sent to me by way of the bailiff, I encourage you to speak freely on the points of this case. This is the time to discuss your concerns. I, of course am looking for a unanimous vote one way or the other. However, in this case, a majority vote works."

He left the jury room and in route to his office he asked the attorneys to join him in his chambers to wait with him.

Both declined. Bradford wanted to wait in the courthouse lockup with her client and Greenwood wanted to have coffee with her team.

They walked to a nearby coffee shop to wait.

They were in the middle of drinking their coffee and discussing the trial when the Court Clerk called Greenwood's cell phone to let her know that the jury was in.

Greenwood paid the tab and they walked together back to the courthouse. When they reached the courtroom, it was so crowded that the overflow spilled into the hall, so she told her team to hold hands like they did as children and she led them through the crowd to the prosecutor's table. The bailiff had roped off the first bench behind the prosecutor's table and winked at them as he undid the rope to let them file in.

When the Courthouse Marshals brought Charlene Bradford and her client, Pablo Castaneda into the courtroom, Bradford's eyes were red and swollen as if she'd been crying. Her client had an arrogant look about him.

The bailiff enter through the side door and called out, "Hear-Ye, Hear-Ye. All rise as The Honorable Gerald Chaney enters the courtroom to hear the jurors verdict for Pablo Castaneda in case number 17-5240, for Money Laundering in violations of Title 18 § 1957."

Judge Chaney said, "Please sit. Has the jury reached a verdict?"

"Yes, Your Honor it has."

"Please hand it to the bailiff."

In turn, the bailiff brought it to the Judge. After reading it, he gave it back to the bailiff who walked it to Foreman who read it aloud, "We the members of the jury for case number 17-4240 charged with Money Laundering in violation, of Title 18 USC § 1957 find the defendant, Pablo Castaneda, guilty of the charge."

There was a stampeded in the courtroom as media rushed to get the news out that Castaneda was found guilty.

There were several who remained behind to hear the sentence the Judge would hand down.

When the courtroom quieted down, Judge Chaney asked, "Will the defendant, Pablo Castaneda, please stand."

Bradford stood with her client; her knees were shacking as she listened to the Judge doled out his sentence of twenty-five years without the benefit of parole.

As Bradford fainted to the floor, she could be heard saying, "I'm a dead woman."

Chapter Twelve

Greenwood's team had some spare time before Craig Morton's trial on Tuesday, April 11, so everyone time to catch up on the home stuff.

Greenwood called her team on Monday evening to let them know that had a jury and the trial was scheduled for tomorrow at 9:00 am in Judge Chaney's courtroom.

Her team met at Jimmy's for breakfast at 7:30 in the morning. They were a quiet group, still on home time.

Nicole paid the breakfast tab and they drove separately to the garage across from the courthouse.

They took the elevator to the 7th floor to find that the courtroom doors were still locked, giving Greenwood the opportunity to let her team know that, "Morton is having his own attorney defend him. The defense attorney's name is Edward O'Conner. I haven't met him yet, but he sounded very professional on the phone.

Morton was less know that Castaneda, so he didn't warrant a big show by the media.

When the bailiff unlocked the doors Greenwood followed by her team into the courtroom. Since Andrea York is a witness to testify in the case, she remained alone in the hall.

The bailiff returned to the courtroom escorting defense attorney Edward O'Conner in with his client, Craig Morton.

Greenwood heard Sophie and Nicole whispering about how good looking O'Connor is. She had a small smile on her face, because she also thought he was good looking.

The bailiff left the courtroom to escort the jurors to the jury box and when they were settled in, he left the courtroom to return though the side door to call out. "Hear-Ye, Hear-Ye. All rise as the Honorable Gerald Chaney enters the courtroom for the trial of Craig Morton in case number 17-5241, for Money Laundering in violation of Title 18 USC § 1957."

When Chaney took his seat on the bench, he asked everyone, "Please sit. Is the Government prepared to present its Opening Summary?"

"Yes, Your Honor, it is."

Greenwood walked to the defense table. "The defendant owns an investment firm and what better is there to have an investment firm have the owner a part of a laundering money scheme. A scheme to not only launder untaxed money, but the money was derived from the sale of drugs. Drugs that were used to poison our young children and the profits then traveled from Baltimore City, Maryland, to Atlantic City, New Jersey, to purchase more drugs. I will present evidence through a witness who actually witnessed the transactions take place. If you agree that we that we need to rid the streets of Baltimore, you must convict the defendant of laundering untaxed drug money."

"Your Honor, the Government has completed its Opening Summary"

"Thank you counselor, the Defense may proceed with its Opening Summary"

"Thank you, Your Honor."

Defense Attorney O'Conner stood and walked straight to the jury box where he looked into the eyes of the jurors intimidating them before speaking. "The Government intimated that my client was threatening the lives of our young children in Baltimore by supplying money to the drug dealers. If that is true, shouldn't my client be charged with drug trafficking? He was not, which means that the charge of Money Laundering is bogus. If you agree with me you must acquit him."

"Your Honor, the defense has concluded its Opening Summary."

With a smirk of success on his face, he spun on one foot to return to the defense table.

It was obvious to everyone in the courtroom that Judge Chaney was not impressed with O'Conner's antics as he said rather tersely that there would be a fifteen minute break before the Government called its witness to the stand.

Greenwood asked Andrea to go into the bathroom while she talked the rest of the team about what to about the defense attorney.

Nicole spoke up, "Andrea will make mince meat out of him."

Greenwood looked at her as she said, "I hope you're right, but we'll have to wait and see."

Greenwood retrieved Andrea from the ladies and said, "Thanks for being such a good sport."

Andrea had no idea what Stacey was talking about, but said "You're welcome."

When Chaney returned to the bench, "The Government may call its witness to the stand."

The Government calls for "Andrea York to take the stand."

The bailiff went out to the hall to retrieve York. He escorted her to the stand and swore her in,

Greenwood stepped forward and asked her to state her name for the record.

York sat tall as she stated, "Andrea Lynn York."

"Ms. York, are you currently employed?"

"Yes ma'am. I am. I work for the Drug Enforcement Agency and it's my responsibility to catalog all incoming drugs and the money from drug sales. It's also my responsibility to search for the source of the money and drugs that I put into a catalog."

Greenwood had York's on the prosecutor's table and as she walked it to the defense attorney, she asked York, Did you write this report?"

"Yes Ma'am, I did."

"Can you share with me and the jury where and how you came about getting the evidence for this report?"

"Do you want me to start at the beginning?"

"Yes, please."

"This case started in Crisfield, Maryland, where two young kids, George Patrick and Harold Simms were running drugs from the eastern shore to the western shore. A married couple was murdered in their sailboat so the two young drug runners used the boat to transport drugs. Members of this team were able take Patrick and Simms into custody. We continued to follow the drugs and were able to watch the drugs and money getting exchanged for the drugs on the corner of a street in Baltimore City, so we followed the cars to see where they bought more drugs. We followed the cars to as service stop, where they passed drugs and money through the car windows, one part of the team follow the drug car back to Baltimore and took the dealers into custody and drove them to the Baltimore Detention Center. My partner, Frank Walden and I followed the money car. Frank and I stayed in the Showboat Casino and Hotel, while two undercover Drug Enforcement agents worked in the Hard Rock Casino and Hotel. The casino owner believed that money was being laundered in his hotel. The undercover DEA agent watched as Pablo Castaneda sat at the casino's bar drinking coffee as he transferred money to off-shore accounts. After we took him into custody, Frank and I confiscated Castaneda's laptop and found three other persons, whose untaxed money was being sent to offshore accounts."

Judge Chaney asked, "Does the defense wish to cross examine this witness?"

"Yes Your Honor, it would."

O'Conner walked to the witness stand and Andrea saw evil in his eyes.

"Ms. York, were my client's fingerprints found on anything?"

"No sir, they were not."

"Did you find his DNA on anything?"

"No sir, I did not."

"In that case, please explain to the jury and me why you are so sure that my client was involved with money laundering charge."

This asshole wasn't going to get the best of her, so she said. "We followed the money. Your client used his business checking account to forward the money to Castaneda with his business EIN."

The evil in his eyes was gone as he said in a quiet voice, "Your Honor, I have no more questions for this witness."

Chaney told her, "Ms. York you may step down."

She smiled at O'Connor as she made her way to sit with her teammates.

The Judge announced, "The court will take a fifteen minute break before we start the closing summations."

The Greenwood team stepped into the as though they needed to stretch their legs. Everyone hugged Andrea and said, "What a great job, you didn't let him to and you sure kicked him in the balls."

At the end of the fifteen minute break everyone returned to the courtroom.

The bailiff enter the courtroom through the side door and called out, "Hear-Ye, Hear-Ye. All rise as the Honorable Gerald Chaney enters the courtroom.

Once he was sitting on the bench, Judge Chaney said, "Everyone may please. The Government may present its closing summation."

Greenwood stood and walked to the defense table. "The defense would have you believe that untaxed money laundering to offshore banks and drug dealing with children who die every day are minor offenses and should be dealt with lightly. If you watch the local news, the number of deaths from drug overdoses and drug wars are reported daily; however, if you agree with the defense that these are minor offenses, you must acquit the defendant. If you find that these are not minor offenses and want drugs out of Baltimore, you have no choice but to find the defendant guilty of the charge of Money Laundering, in violation of Title 18 USC § 1957."

"Thank you Your Honor, the Government has completed its closing summation."

"Thank you counselor, the defense may proceed."

"Thank you, Your Honor."

O'Connor stood and walked to the jury where he said, "The Government's closing summation almost brought tears to my eyes. Let me ask you if you know how one person, namely my client, Craig Morton could have caused that much destruction to the young folks in Baltimore. My client owns a very lucrative investment firm and has no need to deal in either drug trafficking or untaxed off-shore banking."

"Thank you Your Honor, the defense has concluded its closing argument."

"Thank you, Counselor."

Judge Chaney announced, "The bailiff will escort the jury members to the jury room and I'll join you there."

When Chaney entered the jury room, he asked, "By a show of hand do the jury member wish to continue today?"

Every juror raised a hand.

"In that case let me lead you through the process. Amongst yourselves, you will need to appoint a foreman or forewomen who will represent each of you. Any and all questions each of you has will be handed to the bailiff, who will be sitting outside the door and he will bring it to me. This is your time to make sure your concerns are heard by the other jurors. I encourage you to s

Speak freely with one another. In this case a majority vote sets the verdict."

Judge Chaney left the jury room to wait for in verdict in his office.

The Greenwood Team walked to the coffee shop to wait for the verdict.

While sipping on her coffee, Nicole said, "While O'Connor is a good looking man, he's a real buffoon when it comes to the law.

As everyone was agreeing with her, Greenwood's phone rang.

The Judge's Clerk called to tell her that the jury was in.

Greenwood's team filed into a quiet courtroom and sat on the bench behind the prosecutor's table.

The bailiff led the jurors from the jury room to the jury box. Once they were settled in, the bailiff left the courtroom to reenter through the side door to call out, "Hear-Ye, Hear-Ye. All rise as the Honorable Gerald Chaney enters the courtroom.

Once the judge was seated, he said, "Everyone may be seated."

Once everyone in the courtroom was seated, the Judge asked, "Has the jury reached a verdict?"

The foreman stood to say, "Yes Your Honor, it has."

"Please hand to the bailiff."

After reading it, he handed it back to the bailiff, who in turned handed it back to the foreman.

Chaney said, "Will the foreman please read the verdict aloud?"

The foreman stood and said in a clear voice, "We the jurors find the defendant, Craig Morton, guilty of Money Laundering in violation of Title 18 USC § 1957."

The Judge asked, "Will the defendant please stand. I hereby sentence you to twenty-five years without the benefit of parole."

O'Connor stood to address the Judge, "I will request a new trial based on the Government's lies."

Chaney politely said, "You have that option.

He banged his gavel and said, "This court is adjourned.

Chapter Thirteen

There was a week of down time until Monday the 17th, when the jury selection for Bagley Real Estate owner Jack Bagley. The team waited rather nervously in their homes for the call from Greenwood saying, "We have a jury."

When everyone her on the conference call, everyone was relieved.

<>

Greenwood's team met at Jimmy's for breakfast before heading to the courthouse.

During breakfast, Sophie said, "Two down and two to go."

As Nicole paid the breakfast bill, she said, "Sophie, don't be counting your chickens before they hatch."

They drove separately to the parking garage and then walked together to the courthouse.

As they approached the security checkpoint, one of the officers said, "The courthouse is on lockdown, so please turn around and leave the premises immediately."

Once they were through the courthouse doors, and standing on the sidewalk, Nicole sent a text message to Greenwood asking what was going on?

Greenwood texted Nicole back telling them to go to the coffee shop and she would join them as quickly as she could.

Greenwoods team ordered coffee, but sat quietly, unsure what was going on.

Sophie broke the silence by asking, "What does everyone think?"

There was a unanimous shaking of the heads.

Nicole spoke to them, "This has to be real bad if we weren't allowed through the security checkpoint."

Everyone agreed with her statement.

Sophie said, "At least we know Greenwood's alive since she sent the text message."

Nicole wondered out loud, "What if something happened to Judge Chaney?"

The silence at the table was deafening.

Everyone jumped out of their seat when Greenwood entered the café.

She stood to address everyone at the table, "What I'm going to tell you must be silent until the CIA and the FBI can solve what happened and how it happened."

"The defendant, Jack Bagley, murdered his escorts and left in the Detention Center's car. I don't want anyone climbing onto your white horse and go after him. I need all of you to promise me that you won't."

Everyone looked down at the table.

Greenwood said, "This is serious."

Not one member of her team acknowledged that they heard her, so Greenwood said, "At least keep me in the loop."

Everyone nodded that they would.

As Greenwood left the coffee shop, she knew that her team couldn't stay out of it because this was their case and could only hope that they would keep it safe. If anyone could find this bandit, it was her team.

Nicole suggested that they move the meeting to her house to her house and come up with a plan.

<>

Nicole made fresh coffee for everyone and as everyone sat in her living she put their coffee cups on the coffee table along with cream and sugar.

Andrea was the first to speak, "We know that the defendant took the Detention Center's car and probably ditched it somewhere along his route and I think that's where we should start."

Sophie said, "Since we don't know which direction he was going, I can take on the task of call police and tow companies in both directions."

Josh added as a thought, "What are the chances that he caught the first flight out of the US under an alias since he has money stashed around the globe."

Nicole said, "That's a strong possibility, and since Andrea is our chief expert when it comes to money, we're going to make it her task to find where the money went."

Andrea said, "Nicole, if he withdrew the money, there's no way to know where he went."

Nicole told her, "Andrea, we've climbed mountains and forged rivers and streams, so we're not gonna give up this early in the game. You're better than this, tell me who to call and I'll make the calls. We'll work together on this."

Andrea said, "Thanks."

Josh said, "I think that we should get started earlier rather than later and I honestly believe that Andrea should take the lead."

Everyone agreed with Josh.

Andrea said, "We'll get started in the morning after a good night of sleep, but to recap tonight's meeting, Sophie will take charge of finding the car. Nicole will call the airports, train and bus stations. Josh, I'm going to depend on you to keep track of this motley crew to keep them going in the right direction."

"I can do that."

Everyone said their good-nights as well as thanking Nicole for hosting this meeting.

<>

Everyone showed up on time at Jimmy's to get started on their new project of finding Jack Bagley.

Andrea paid the breakfast bill and then everyone left to do their part in this investigation.

Sophie hit pay dirt right with the first call. The car had been towed to Baltimore's Forensic Vehicle lab and no one had examined it yet. It was a short drive to the lab.

She parked her car on the lot, went to Office to sign the log. The duty officer told her, "Agent Brock, no one has been near the car, so she's all yours. Let me know if you need anything."

"I will."

Sophie took her forensic kit with her to the car. She set the kit on the floor and walked around the exterior of the car assessing it for any damage such as dents, broken glass or flat tires. She found nothing that warranted her concern. It was time to check out the interior of the car, so she pulled her gloves on and grabbed her finger print kit. She found a great deal of blood, so she backed out of the car to get her sample kit, she labeled each sample and put each sample into a bag for the forensic lab in the ME's lab.

As she moved to the back seat, her body shook all over. She found a pair of handcuffs with the key along with what appeared to be a homemade bloody knife.

Sophie bagged everything and made her way to the City's Morgue where the Forensic lab was located. She handed over everything she had and asked the technician to examine everything.

He asked, "Agent Brock, I'm pretty backed up, can you come back tomorrow and I'll have everything done for you."

Sophie told him, "I'm sorry, but I can't because we're looking for man who murdered two Baltimore Detention Center's drivers."

"In that case, I'll start on this now."

"Thank you, I'll wait for your results."

She stepped outside the building to call Andrea, "Andrea, in collecting evidence from the car, I found handcuffs with the key along with a bloody homemade knife, which leads me to believe that another inmate gave our bandit what he needed to escape."

"Andrea, I'm heading to the Detention Center and see what I can learn."

"Sophie, I don't think that's a good idea."

"I'll give you a call later and let you know what I learned."

"Sophie, I'm not keen on this plan."

"Neither am I, but if I get answers, it will be worth it. I don't believe that I'll be in physical risk, but I'm more than sure that the officials will accuse me of lying.

Sophie drove to the Detention Center where she parked on the lot and cautiously entered the building.

She told the duty officer, "My name is Sophie Brock; I'm a FBI Agent and would like to speak with Warden Charles Thompson.

"In reference to what Agent Brock?"

"Two of the Detention Center's drivers were murdered while in transit for a trial and I would like to speak with Warden Thompson about what I uncovered."

He picked up the phone, "I need an escort for FBI Agent to the Warden's Office."

The escort tapped on the warden's door and then opened it for Agent Brock to enter the office.

Once inside the office, Sophie thought that Warden Thompson was one fine looking man, who could lead her astray if she wasn't careful.

"Agent Brock, what can I do for you?"

Before saying anything, she pulled the bags out, one contained the handcuffs with the key and the other contained the homemade bloody knife.

"I found these in the backseat of the transport car driven by Samuel Paxton and co-piloted by Benjamin Sadowski for Jack Bagley, who was on his way to the Federal Courthouse for his trial."

"Agent Brock, am I to assume that one of our guards provided these to your defendant?"

Sophie said, "No, I wouldn't make any assumption as to who provided these to Bagley; I can only tell you that the FBI certainly did not."

"In that case, it had to be another inmate."

"That was my assumption when I recovered the bloody handmade knife."

"Agent Brock, I can't let you walk out the door without telling you 'thank you'."

Sophie smiled as she said, "You're welcome."

He asked her, "Is there a chance that you can keep me up to date on this bandit over a cup of coffee?"

"I would like that."

Sophie called Andrea before she pulled off the lot

"It went really well, so where do you want me to go now?"

"I don't have a new task for you just yet; Nicole and I are working on the money."

"Get any leads?"

"As a matter of fact yes, we found a transfer to the Greek Isles, so I called Interpol, the international agency to give us a hand."

Sophie said, "Wow, that's big!"

"It is and I can only hope they'll take him into custody and bring him home."

Judge Chaney called Stacey Greenwood and asked, "Is your team work to find Bagley?"

"Your Honor told us not to look for him."

"Have they learned anything yet?"

"Your Honor, no one has said a word to me because you told them to let the FBI handle it."

"Who's leading your team of investigators?"

"Andrea York."

"Counselor, please call her and see where they are in this investigation because I need to know whether to sit tight or move on to the Barns' trial."

"Your Honor, I'll call her as soon as we disconnect this call."

Greenwood called Andrea and told her, "Chaney called me and wants to know where we are on the Bagley case so he can decide to move on to the Barns' case or sit tight on the Bagley case."

"I'm waiting to hear back from Interpol. We believe Bagley took his money and fled to the Greek Isles. Can Judge Chaney give us two days before he makes a decision?'"

"I'll call and ask him, and then I'll call you back."

"Stacey, before you go, who told Judge Chaney that we are working on the case?"

"The Judge is not a stupid man, he knows how attached you are to this case."

It was only a few minutes before Greenwood called Andrea and told her, "Judge Chaney said to keep moving forward on the Bagley case."

"Thanks boss, I was hoping you would say that because we are so frigging close to nabbing him."

After they disconnected the call, Stacey chuckled because she'd never heard Andrea come close to cursing.

Andrea set up a conference call to tell them that, "Judge Chaney said to keep working on the Bagley case."

Sophie asked, "Who told him that we were working on the case?"

"Sophie, he knows us and knew that regardless of what he said, this is our case and we want to finish it."

She could hear everyone on the phone say, "That's right."

Now that the team knew that Judge Chaney had faith in them, they were becoming frustrated waiting for Interpol to call, but they stayed in touch and kept moving forward to keep the tension down.

It was becoming a chore to get through each day without a call from Interpol.

The call finally came in and Andrea was so excited that could barely talk, she managed to say to the team, "Interpol called, they have Bagley in custody and would deliver him to the Baltimore Detention Center.

Andrea then called Greenwood with the news who in turn called Judge Chaney.

Judge Chaney said, "I'll issue the arrest warrant for Premeditated Murder to take with you to the Detention Center when you read him his Miranda Rights for the new charge of First Degree Murder in violation of Title 18 US Code § 1111.

Greenwood drove to the Detention Center, signed in and then sat across the interview table and read Bagley his Miranda right as she asked him to sign the form; she asked him if he understood his rights?"

He said, "I understand them."

Greenwood pulled the warrant out of her briefcase and said, "I have a warrant to serve you for First Degree Murder in violation of Title 18 US Code § 1111."

"Mr. Bagley, may I ask why you did it?"

He told her honestly, "The money I sent off-shore was my retirement money."

"Mr. Bagley, why did you kill the two escorts in the car?"

"Can I tell you this confidentially?"

"No you can't Mr. Bagley because I'm the Prosecutor in this case which means anything you say to me I can use against you in the courtroom."

"I understand, but let me say, if I'm convicted of the murder charge and from what I've heard you're a great prosecutor, which means I'll be convicted and land in prison. I've designated the money to go to my girlfriend in Greece."

Greenwood wondered if he was going for an insanity plea, but she wasn't buying into it, so she said, "Mr. Bagley, I'll see you in the courtroom. Before I leave, do you have an attorney to represent you?"

"Yes, his name is Aaron Graham."

Greenwood drove back to the courthouse and walked directly to Chaney Office. Without knocking she opened the door and walked in.

"Your Honor he has an attorney and is ready to be arraigned."

"Stacy, are you okay?"

"Yes Your Honor, I am, so let's get this show on the road."

Chaney told her, "I haven't heard a peep from the media which means it knows nothing about Bagley being in custody, so this might be a quick trial. Please calls the US Marshals office to have a deputy deliver him to the courthouse in leg irons as well as hand cuffs on his back and last, I want him dressed in his undergarments so he can't hide keys or knives."

The US Marshal's Office was one floor down, so rather than call, she took the steps down the one level and when she entered the office she said, "Judge Chaney has ordered this. He wants Deputy US Marshals to collect Jack Bagley from the Detention Center and deliver him to the courthouse in leg iron as well as hand cuff in his undergarments."

Deputy Grant Young asked, "Stacey, are you serious?

"Unfortunately I am. Jack Bagley is the guy that murdered the two escorts who were taking him to the courthouse. They're names are Clark Albert and Joshua Bayard."

Deputy US Marshal Sam Wadsworth said, "I remember that case. How did you find him?"

"Interpol found him in Greece and escorted him to the Baltimore Detention Center."

"We'll find two guys to cover the desk and we'll pick him up, because no one in this department would believe us if they were told how to pick him up.

His attorney, Aaron Graham was in the conference room with his client when the Deputy US Marshals arrived to transport him to the courthouse.

Deputy US Marshal Young asked Bagley, "Undress to your skivvies."

Graham was angry and made it known, "Someone is going pay for this humiliation to his client."

He stuffed Bagley's street clothes into a bag and followed the Deputy Marshals to the courthouse shouting obscenities out the window all the way to the courthouse.

Once he was secure in the courthouse cell, he pulled his now wrinkled suit from the bag and dressed in front of his attorney and two Deputy Marshals, humiliated that he had to do this in front of them.

The bailiff arrived to check on Bagley's progress in getting dressed.

When the bailiff saw that Bagley was fully dressed, he escorted the defendant and his attorney, Aaron Graham into the defense table.

Greenwood sat at the prosecutor's table with the majority of her team sitting on the bench behind her. Agents Sophie Brock waited in the hall to testify if the need arose

The bailiff came through the side door to call out, "Hear-Ye, Hear-Ye. All rise as the Honorable Gerald Chaney enters the courtroom to hear testimony in case Number 5144 in First Degree Murder in violation of Title 18 US Code § 1111."

As Chaney sat on the bench, "He asked everyone to please sit. Next, he asked the defendant to stand"

His attorney Aaron Graham stood as well.

Judge Chaney did not request a jury for this case; because he would preside over the case.

He asked the defendant, "How do you plea?"

"Your Honor, I have no choice, but to plead guilty of the charge. My only request is that the money I laundered remains in Greece and be giving to Laura Sachet, who is my girlfriend."

Judge Chaney told the defendant. "I now have no control over the money you laundered because this case regards the murder charges. I'm sentencing you to two life sentences without the benefit of parole."

Aaron Graham stood to address the Bench, "Your Honor, I'm lodging a complaint as to the way my client was handled by two Deputy Marshals, who asked him to strip down to his skivvies."

The Judge said, "That was done under my directive."

Chapter Fourteen

The last case to be heard in this series of was for Joseph Barns, owner of Barns Yachts case number for Money Laundering.

His defense lawyer, Bethany Stromberg, sat with her client in the Detention Center until she was called to the courthouse for jury selection. Her client was crying his heart out. Stromberg sat with him to stop his crying, but he would have none of it.

He finally managed to blubber out, "I have thrown away my life and would leave my family penniless."

Beth asked him, "Joe what did you spend the money on?"

Still blubbering, he said "I gambled it all away and was hoping to win it back. I won't be able to pay it back now."

"Joe, I need to go to the courthouse for the jury selection, but I'll stop in afterward to let you know how it went."

"Thank you Ms. Stromberg. I'll be here waiting to hear from you."

She drove to the courthouse where she met Stacey Greenwood for the first time, thinking that Greenwood looked confident in her stature and it intimidated her.

They entered the courtroom together and sat side by side in chairs waiting for the judge to get started.

Judge Chaney entered the courtroom to stand in front of the bench to explain to the forty folks looking at him, "Did everyone get a number from the Clerk's office?"

Everyone held the card up with the number not facing the judge.

"That's good. The prosecutor will call out a random number, will the prosecutor please hold up a hand?"

Greenwood held up her hand thinking the judge didn't want another mishap in his courtroom.

Judge Chaney then explained to the forty folks looking at him. "The procedure for selecting a jury is that the Government will call out a number and if it's your number, please stand and answer the question honestly. The Defense Attorney will ask the same number a different question and before we begin the attorney's must agree on fourteen jurors. Two of the fourteen will be alternate jurors in the event a juror cannot complete the task."

The Government looked over the faces and called out. "Will number 14 please stand?"

A young woman stood, she was about 5'6" tall with auburn colored hair, looking as though she wanted to be anywhere else and not here.

The Government asked, "Do you attend college?"

"Yes ma'am I do."

The defense attorney asked, "What is your major?"

"I'm studying to be a large animal veterinarian."

They each took a turn questioning potential until Chaney called for a one-hour lunch break.

The Bailiff escorted the prospective jurors to the jury room where lunch was waiting for them.

Greenwood and Stromberg dined in Judge Chaney's chambers.

They handed their lists to him and, he said, "Never in my years of sitting on the bench have I seen a complete match of number this early in the day. Please tell me that you did not somehow, someway agree on this list."

Greenwood and Stromberg looked at one another and Greenwood said, "Great minds think alike."

Chaney said, "Yea right. I'm going into the jury room and instruct them on the process; first you need to appoint a foreman or forewoman along with two alterative, along with submitting questions to me through the bailiff."

When Chaney returned to his chambers, he shook his head, while saying, "Looks like we have a jury, so I'll see the both of you in the morning."

Stromberg drove to the Detention Center to let her client know that his trial would begin tomorrow morning. The news of the trial brought a new round of his crying.

Greenwood set up a conference call to notify her team that they had a jury and the Barns case was on deck for tomorrow morning.

<>

Greenwood's team met for breakfast at Jimmy's in Fells Point.

During breakfast Sophie said, "I hope this gets done smoothly."

As she paid the breakfast tab, Nicole said, "I think we all do."

They drove separately to the parking lot, but walked together as a team to the courthouse. As they passed the security checkpoint Sophie said, "Well, at least we made it this far."

Nicole chuckled, "You're right."

Greenwood was waiting in the hall for the bailiff to unlock the courtroom doors.

While they waited, Greenwood told Andrea, "I'm not sure what to expect in the courtroom and as my primary witness, would you please wait in the hall until I know what's going on?"

"It's not a problem for me. Just don't forget that I'm in the hall."

Greenwood told her, "I won't forget that you're in the hall."

Greenwood took her seat at the prosecutor's with her non testifying team members on the bench behind her.

The bailiff escorted Bethany Stromberg and her client, Joseph Barns to sit at the defense table

Stromberg and Greenwood exchanged looks because Barns' eyes were read and swollen.

The bailiff then escorted the jury in and left through the side door and returned through the same side doo to announce, "Hear-Ye, Hear-Ye. All rise as the Honorable Gerald Chaney enters the courtroom for the trial of Joseph Barnes in case number 17-5143, for Money Laundering in violation of Title 18 USC § 1957"

Barnes stood to address the Judge. He started to cry. "Your Honor, I would like to change my plea to guilty"

Greenwood sent Sophie to collect Andrea from the hall.

Judge Chaney had never encountered this before, so he asked the defendant why he wanted to change his plea.

Barnes started to cry, "Your Honor, I laundered the money and threw it away gambling leaving my family penniless."

"Mr. Barnes, you leave me no choice, but to sentence you to twenty-five years in prison. I'm going to suggest that you take advantage of the prison's Gambling Anonymous program."

Chaney then announced while banging his gavel, "This court is adjourned."

As they left the courtroom, Greenwood asked Stromberg to join her team for dinner at the BLACKWALL Hitch restaurant on Pratt Street.

"Thank you for the invite. I'll meet you there."

Greenwood secured a table where everyone could sit with a view out the window.

Stromberg sat across the table from Greenwood.

After the beverages were delivered, Greenwood stood to announce, "The dinner tab is complements of US Attorney Theodor Chennault. He said, 'There wasn't a better team.'"

Bethany asked, "Should I plan to pay for my dinner?"

Stacy told her, "Hell no."

Nicole asked, "Is this the end of our team?"

"To tell you the truth, I'm not sure; however, this a great team, so I see something coming into our future."

Nicole said, "Since Barns was so upset I'm afraid he's going to commit suicide in prison."

The author was born and raised in Baltimore County, Maryland. Her family sailed ever summer in and out of the rivers on the Chesapeake Bay.

Fells Point, Maryland was a port for schooners that brought fresh vegetables from the eastern shore to the western shore. The fastest schooner received the highest price for its cargo.

That tradition is still alive through schooner participants in the Great Chesapeake Bay Schooner Race

Other Books by Denise Irwin

Johnny

The Pink Chestnut

Alison

Bartholomew

Cassandra

The Cherry Blossoms

Donna

Elijah

Frieda

Gabin

Ian

Kaitlyn

Broken

Things That Happen in the Night

- I wish you enough sun to keep your attitude bright no matter how gray the day may appear.
- I wish you enough rain to appreciate the sun even more.
- I wish you enough happiness to keep your spirit alive and everlasting.
- I wish you enough pain so that even the smallest of joys in life may appear bigger.
- I wish you enough gain to satisfy your wanting.
- I wish you enough loss to appreciate all that you possess.
- I wish you enough hellos to get you through the final good-bye
- He began to cry and walked away
- They say it takes a minute to find a special person, a day to love them; but then an entire life to forget them

Anonymous